SOCK SAGA

By:

Philip J. Barlett

Published by Book Writing Pioneer

Cover design by Book Writing Pioneer

ISBN: Printed in the United States

barlett71@yahoo.com

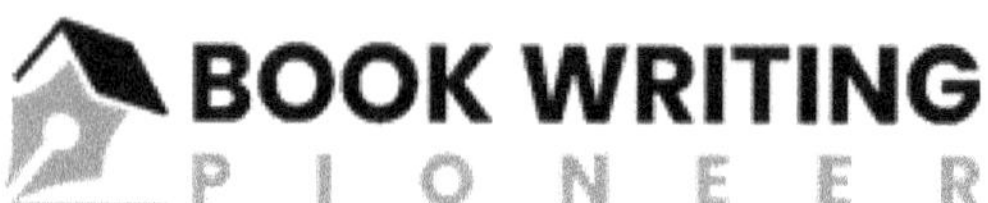

TABLE OF CONTENTS

CHAPTER 1
THE GATHERING

The front door closed with a thud. Slowly, a green sock with three red diamonds on his head opened his eyes. Seeing that the coast was clear, he stood up. *Finally! The last human had left for the day*, he thought.

"Darla!" he called out, "Let's go."

"I'm coming, Dart," she replied. The other green sock with three red diamonds, who was her pair, walked up to him.

"The humans were running late today," she said.

"Yeah, they were. I thought the boy was going to stay home from school again."

They entered the hallway and heard their names being called. Dashing towards them was a green and yellow sock named "Jet." He talked fast and was always on the move. He was the most excitable of the bunch.

"Guess what? I have an idea for going outside!" Jet blurted out in his usual quick manner.

Before Dart and Darla could react, he started telling them his idea.

"You see, we have to go and..." Jet droned on and on. He was always thinking of an idea to do something different. This time, it was going next door to the other house.

"So, what do you think?"

"Huh?" said Dart, missing most of what Jet said. "Oh, uh, I think it's great." He continued.

"Thank you," said Jet, running off. "I have to tell the others."

"Dart, do you like the idea?" asked Darla.

Dart just shrugged. "I think it's a great idea but a dangerous one too. So much could go wrong. First, we will have to find a way to get outside. I think it's pretty much impossible. I would love to go out and explore, walk through the grass, touch and climb trees, but the door and windows are always closed. And if they were somehow left open, we'd be spotted for sure," he continued.

"Well, then," said Darla, cutting in. "Maybe you should work with Jet!"

They walked into the sister's bedroom. There, they saw some of the others.

"Meg! Marty!" Darla called out. Two black and yellow socks whirled around.

"Heyyyyy, you two!! How are you doing?" Marty asked.

"We are okay. We just talked with Jet," replied Dart. "Or rather, *HE* did all the talking."

"I don't know how Jade puts up with him," Marty chuckled.

"Well, I do admire Jet for always wanting to better us," Meg added. "I'm actually excited about the possibility of going outside to visit other socks." Her eyes got big with excitement of possibly getting out in the world.

Just then, a herd of dust bunnies went by, hopping in the next room.

"Ahh!!! The life of a dust bunny," said Marty.

"No worries at all. They just hop around. Except when the mom cleans," said Meg.

"Then all those poor dust bunnies disappear. Never to be seen again." They all shuddered

"Speaking of cleaning," Dart began with a serious voice, "tomorrow is laundry day. We must hide."

They all nodded. The other socks relied on Dart to keep a schedule. He was a thinker and their unofficial leader. All the socks came to him for advice. Darla especially. She couldn't have had a better mate. Dart seemed to always have an answer and kept them safe. Laundry day was a sock's biggest fear. They all heard tales of socks disappearing in either the washer or the dryer, never to be seen again. To prevent this, all the socks held on to each other for safety, but the risk was still there. Many mates over many years have disappeared. The laundry room was the most feared place in the house. No sock even went near it, but all the socks in the house were familiar with how the machines worked, so even though they feared them, they knew how to take precautions.

Even though they all hide the best they can to avoid getting washed and dried, some socks got found. Sometimes, they all got found. If a sock ever got found without its mate, other socks immediately would try to team up and hold hands, but disaster would strike every now and then, leaving the socks more scared. Just then, it began to rain. Dart looks out of the window.

"We had better leave," Dart instructed the group. "The father comes home early whenever it rains."

The socks didn't move when humans were around. Only when the humans were away would they roam and run around free, hold meetings, and talk about plans to go outside, most of which were risky and dangerous. As Dart and Darla were about to leave the room, Dart stopped and took another look out of the window for a brief moment. He hopefully looked at the other house, which looked so far away.

"Maybe soon, we can follow Jet's plan," said Darla, walking down the hall. "If we can understand it, that is," she patted Dart's back and smiled.

"Yeah," answered Dart. "It would be fun. Maybe we can be free one day."

"Free!" Darla exclaimed. "Free to roam around without worrying about disappearing."

"Free!" Dart joined in. "FuhREEE," he sang off-key.

Darla chuckled. "Oh, Dart, you always make me laugh."

"Well, that's my purpose in life," Dart answered back. "To make you laugh and be happy."

"I'm tired of living with humans. There's surely more to do out there," he said, motioning to the outside.

"One day, we will find out," Darla said excitedly and with hope. "And we will find out together," she added as she held Dart's hand.

"We will always be together, Darla," Dart assured, gripping her hand.

"But what if we ever got separated, Dart? I couldn't go on," Darla replied.

Dart shook his head. "No matter what, our bond will always have us find our way to each other," he reassured Darla and took another one of her hands in his own. Just then, a car stopped outside the house, and the voice of the door opening and the mom's and kid's footsteps were heard and got louder by the second. Darla and Dart made a run back to the room and slid to their hiding spots.

CHAPTER 2
DISAPPEARING DART

The next day, the mother started grabbing the laundry. "Come on, kids," she said. "Give me all your dirty clothes."

Dart and Darla scrunched inside a shoe. It was a good place. They had hidden many times before. "Just be quiet," Dart whispered to Darla. "We should be fine."

"There's a pair of pants," said the boy. Just when he was about to stuff the pants into the basket and take them to the laundry, he noticed some of Dart sticking out of the shoe. "I better grab the sock also," he said. Dart and Darla froze at what the boy said. Dart pushed Darla a little harder inside the shoe to make sure she wasn't seen by the boy and didn't get grabbed. Darla was scared for Dart and herself. For a brief moment, they couldn't hear the boy. They thought he had left.

Dart and Darla relaxed for a little while, and Dart smiled to calm Darla down. Just then, a swoosh of a hand came and snatched Dart out of the shoe. Darla tried to hang on tight to Dart but couldn't. Before exiting the shoes, he made Darla lose his hands to save her from being seen.

Grabbing Dart, the boy shoved Dart into the basket with the rest of the clothes. The blue jeans felt heavy on Dart, who struggled to keep his head out of the pile of clothes to watch Darla and see whether she was safe or not. Dart could only look with panic at Darla peeking out of the shoe. The boy gave his mother the clothes.

"OK," says the mom. "Make sure you do your chores. I'll be back soon."

Covered in clothes, Dart starts moving in the basket. "Is anyone here?" he whispers.

Nobody answered.

"Oh well, I should be fine!" Dart said to himself. "It's the laundry room."

The mom begins loading the baskets in the car. Puzzled, Dart looks around through the holes in the basket. *This isn't the laundry room,* he thought. The mother starts driving. Soon, she pulls up to a building and brings the baskets inside. Dart looked around in awe at the gleaming pile of washers and dryers. The mother puts the clothes down and walks off. Dart sees another sock peeking out of the other basket. It was Terry, Jet's friend.

"Terry, are you alone?" he whispers.

"Yeah! I'm glad to see you, Dart."

"We meet in the middle of the washer like normal, right?"

"Right," said Dart, giving the thumbs-up.

Just then, the mother comes back and starts loading the clothes in the washing machine. As agreed, Dart and Terry move to the middle and hold hands. It was a move that a sock learns when it's created. It's harder to disappear if socks are joined together.

"Terry," said Dart, "I was unlucky this time. He found me."

"What about Darla?" asked Terry.

"She was left behind," Dart replied.

Just then, the clothes started spinning. The socks were no longer being washed with an agitator in the middle. They were now vertical in a metal drum.

"This is different, Terry," said Dart.

"Yeah, I don't like it either, Dart," Terry replied.

Just then, the washer door opened.

"I can't believe I forgot the sneakers," they heard the mother say.

She throws in a pair of sneakers. Now Terry and Dart had to contend with those also.

"Sneakers? Really," Terry said.

The sneakers started clunking around. Dart and Terry were doing their best to avoid them. Finally, a sneaker hits their hands, knocking them apart. The sneaker then smacks into Dart, knocking him close to the edge.

"No!" Dart cries out, trying to get around the sneaker. "Terry, help me!!"

"Dart, hold on! I'm coming," he heard Terry say.

Just then, the sneaker slams into Dart again, causing everything to go black and pushing him through the edge.

"Dart!" Yells Terry.

But there was no answer. Just the sound of sneakers clunking. It was all Terry could do to avoid them. Just when Terry thought the sneakers would hit him, the washer stopped. The mother started pulling the clothes out. Terry was put in the basket. He was watching and hoping to see Dart. But Dart was nowhere to be found. Terry dreaded having to tell the others.

After drying the clothes, the mother left the laundromat and drove home. She put the cleaned clothes in the laundry room. That night, when everyone was asleep, Terry left the basket to go to the guest room. The rule was that a sock who goes to get washed always goes there to meet back up with their mate. He sees Tilly by the door.

"Oh, Tilly!" Terry wailed. "Dart's gone."

"Wait, What!?? Dart is gone? Noooo!" Tilly moaned, horrified.

"Yes, it's true."

"Oh, how I dread telling Darla"! Terry walked into the room with a heavy heart.

He saw Jet, Jade, Meg, and Marty among the others.

Darla was anxiously waiting. "Terry, where's Dart?" she asked.

Just then, Terry sinks to his knees, hands covering his tear-filled face.

"Darla!" he gasps, "Dart is gone!"

"What?" Darla screams. "No... no... please say you're kidding," she asked. "Terry, it's not funny," she called out.

"No, I'm not kidding," said Terry.

"He was knocked into the unknown. We were holding hands and the mother put sneakers in the machine! She's never done that! The sneaker slammed into Dart, and I... I tried to help!! Really, I did!!" he sobbed, not looking up.

"No! no! no! no!" screamed Darla. "This is the most horrible joke! Right? Is it a joke??" Her voice wavered.

Darla choked back a sob. But just looking at Terry, Darla knew it was no joke. She had truly lost her mate. Darla sank to her knees, crying uncontrollably. The other socks immediately rushed to comfort her. And they knew they had to protect her. But unfortunately, it's a reality that when a sock loses its mate, the owner usually throws the other out, never to be seen again. They all heard the stories, and it frightened every sock.

"Darla," Jade says softly, "You should stay with Jet and I. Just stay in the corner behind the bedpost in the sister's room. No one ever looks there." Darla could only nod sadly as she walked off with Jet and Jade. She held their hands tightly. The other socks just stood there, still not believing Dart was gone.

CHAPTER 3
DARLA'S PLAN

A few days went by. It was business as usual in the house. The Mom got the kids ready for school. The father had already left. Soon, the mother would also leave. The socks all milled around, talking in hushed tones. The news about Dart reached all the socks. They all came to cheer Darla up, but all Darla did was stare straight ahead. The other socks feared she would never snap out of it. She was taking the loss hard, but at the same time, she was trying to figure out how to find Dart. Jet and Jade tried to make her smile. Meg and Marty also tried. But to no avail. Darla just stared. The hours went by.

Darla then smiled.

"Okay, you smiled," said Jet. "That's a start."

"Well," Darla began, "I know what I need to do. I must find Dart."

Right away, the others disagreed.

"It's too dangerous," said Jet.

"It's too reckless," said Jade.

As for Meg and Marty, they both said they would do the same as her if faced with the same choice. Darla decided to visit Old Betsy and Billy. Two yellow socks. They were the oldest socks in the house. They were the father's great-grandfather's socks. They were called family heirlooms, so therefore, they were safe. They loved to entertain the other socks with stories of days long ago. Darla went to the bedroom where they were kept.

"Well, look who it is! It's Darla," said Betsy.

"Who?" Billy yelled.

"Darla, you old coot!" replied Betsy.

"Oh, Darla, please come here," Billy said. "We heard all about Dart. We are sorry it happened."

"Thank You," replied Darla.

"Well, what brings you here?" Betsy asked.

"First, I'm sorry I haven't visited in a while," said Darla. "It's just Dart…"

"Oh, hush!" said Betsy, cutting her off. "We understand."

"I wanted to ask you a question," Darla replied.

"Sure," Billy said. "What is it?"

"Well," Darla began, "I want to know if it's possible to come back from the unknown. Or maybe for a sock to go to the unknown and find their mate?"

"Well... it's possible," said Billy.

"No! It's not!" Betsy countered.

"It's foolhardy! What about Ellie?" Billy asked.

"Oh, Ellie!" said Betsy, "So full of tales and imagination. Poor child, she was eccentric."

Darla was curious. "Who's Ellie?"

Billy looked down. "A sock Betsy and I knew many years ago. She was in a dryer and claimed she got knocked through the crack and held on for dear life," said Billy.

"Anyway," Betsy continued, eyes narrowing, "just when she couldn't hold on much longer, the dryer stopped. She grabbed onto a shirt and got pulled back out. But she claimed she saw lights far below. We all laughed at her, but she was insistent. One day, she made up her mind to go through the crack. Naturally, us and others tried to stop her, but we couldn't. One day, she just left. Never to be seen again."

"Well, maybe she made it," said Darla.

"No," said Betsy. "It's called the 'unknown' for an obvious reason. Get the idea out of your head, child. Stay where it's safe." "Thank you to both of you, but it is what I need to do," Darla said.

"If you must go," said Billy, "take something that belonged to Ellie."

"Oh, that's right," said Betsy. "I'll get it."

Going behind the drawer, she had a silver string. "This belonged to her," said Billy.

"She said this would be her goal to come back. Maybe you will find her."

Billy then hugs her! "You be careful," he said, eyes glistening.

Betsy then hugs her. "We will miss you. Remember what we taught you. Be brave! And always stay alert."

"Thanks," you both said Darla, "I'll miss you too. But I need to find Dart."

The next day was laundry day. Darla knew what she had to do. All night, the other socks tried to stop her, but she was determined. That morning, mother was filling baskets. Darla waited. Seeing her chance, she jumped into the basket. The sister picked up the basket.

"Do you have them?" asked mother.

"Yes, this is all of them," the sister replied.

"Good, the thrift store can use them."

Thrift store? Darla wondered. *What was that?*

The baskets were loaded into the car, and the mother drove off.

"Is anyone here?" Darla whispered.

There was only silence. Finally, the car stopped. Mother went to a metal box and threw the basket with Darla in it. Darla climbed out and looked around. There was only darkness.

How will I get to the laundry room now? She wondered. She started to climb over piles of junk. She reached the top and looked out. Just then, her eyes grew heavy.

"What's happening?" Darla mumbled as she fell asleep.

CHAPTER 4
DART'S NEW WORLD

Dart landed with a thud, and then everything went black again.

"Terrr… My hand!... Grabbbb!!! Darlaaa… hide!" he muttered with his eyes closed.

"Daaaaarrrtt, I am cominggg!" Terry's words came from the darkness.

Dart swung his hands, trying to grab onto something. His eyes were closed. Then suddenly, a whole wave of water came crashing over him.

Splaassshhh!!

"What… What happened?" he groaned. He saw he was lying on some green dirt. Slowly getting up, he looked around. He saw bunches of trees and bushes.

"This looks like outside!" He paused to see more, and he realized he really was outside. *Woah! I'm outside!* He thought. He got excited, and his heart started thumping inside him. He was happy for a moment but thought, *But... How?* He looked around again. "Hello?" he called out. No one replied. The only sound that came was that of the flapping of a bird's wings. He looked up. Just then, a bird flew by him; it was made of dust, like the bunnies in his and Darla's room. He ducked, scared that the bird might try to grab him again, and then looked up at the bird again. *A dust... bird?* he thought. Dart slowly started walking. He was scared and amazed at the same time. "Terry? Jet? Marty? Darla? Meg?... anyone?" he whimpered. He was being careful not to be seen by anyone, at least not by the bird that was hovering above. This was his first time out and alone, and the bird looked menacing with its sharp beak and claws.

He called out his friends again, but there were only the sounds of the forest around him. No Darla, no Marty, no Jet. As Dart was moving, he heard a rustling of the leaves and grass around him.

"Who is it?" he asked with a loud voice.

He didn't want to look scared to anyone who was around. But he was frightened. He heard the rustling again, so he sped up and started walking faster, almost at a jogger's pace. He occasionally called out but never received an answer. After another hour of walking, Dart called out a final time. "Hello? Is anyone here?"

"Yeah!" a gravelly voice answered back.

"I'm here." A weak voice called out.

Dart couldn't see anyone around. He froze. He started recalling all the dreadful things he had heard about going outside. Suddenly, the bushes started rustling. Dart decided that if it was an animal, he would just run back in the same direction he had come from. The bushes rustled again, and Dart was about to dash away when suddenly two socks jumped out, scaring Dart cold. One was cream-colored, and the other one was black with green stripes.

"Who are you?" asked Dart, relieved to see it was two socks just like him.

He was also happy to learn he finally found someone he could talk to. Maybe they could help him with some guidance on how he can return home.

"We are the boogey socks," the cream-colored one threatened. He slowly started to walk towards Dart with squinted eyes and hands raised above his head. "We came to eat you." He added without moving his eyes away from Dart.

"No!" screamed Dart and took a few steps back. He was secretly looking for a stick or a stone or anything he could use to scare the threat away. "Leave me alone!"

"Whoa," said the black and green sock. "He is kidding. Why would you say that, Sal? Don't mind him!"

"I don't know," Sal replied. "I couldn't help it." He added and gave a friendly pat on Dart's back. "Relax, pal, we are friends!"

"Anyway," the black and green sock said, "My name is Sol, and that is Sal."

"I'm... Dart," Dart replied cautiously but confidently. "Where am I? I must get back to the dryer."

"Oh! Oh!" said Sol excitedly. "So you came from the other world. How was it? Was it exciting?" Sol asked question after question.

"The other world?" asked Dart.

"Yeah," said Sal. "You are just outside of East Sockton. You are in a new world!"

"You mean this," said Dart, waving his arm around, "is the unknown? I'm in the unknown!! I'll never see Darla again." He cried, covering his face with his hands.

"Hey! Calm down," said Sal, holding Dart by the shoulders. "It's okay... deep breaths; you can do it! Just calm yourself down friend; no need to panic!"

Dart eased a little at Sal's reassurance and started breathing normally again, wiping his tears.

"See! Stay calm," Sal added and kept a hand on his shoulder.

Dart said. "I need to sit down."

"Sure, sit down," said Sol.

Dart sat on a log. "That's better," he said. He looked up at Sal and Sol. "I have questions... Are there other socks here? Also, do you know how I can go back to where I came from?" The two socks saw that Dart was very eager to go home and was clearly distressed.

"No," said Sal. "Just us three. We are the only three here."

Dart cried out, wide-eyed.

"No," said Sol. "There are countless socks!" He was a bit agitated at Sal for being funny when Dart was in trouble and panicked

"But you said there were only three of us," Dart remarked, confused and angry.

"Oh," laughed Sal. "I thought you meant right here in this spot."

"Okay," said Dart. He understood that if there was someone who could help him get back home and to Darla, it would be these two, so he decided to calm his panic and make friends with them. "How do you two know each other? Are you mates?" he asked.

"No, we aren't mates," Sal replied. "I was wandering around like you some years ago, and I ran into Sol. We hit it off and became friends."

"So, you are also lost," Dart replied. "Don't you miss your mates?"

"Well," Sol began, "I don't remember my mate. I did at first." Dart saw Sol sigh a little. He also seemed sad.

"I don't remember mine either," Sal added. "In time, you lose ties to the other world." He shrugged his shoulders and smiled. "What was your mate like, Dart?" Sal asked.

"Darla?" replied Dart. He suddenly had a smile on his face. "Darla is amazing. She is smart and resourceful, and she just makes you feel good around her. And I have friends, Jet, Jade, Meg, Marty, and others. Jet always rambled on and on, and we just rolled our eyes. He was working on a plan to get us outside. But how I wish I could hear him now. I miss everyone," said Dart, tears welling up in his eyes again. "I must get back there."

"I'm sorry, Dart. It hurts," Sol said softly, patting Dart's shoulder. "Look at it this way. You are outside now. This Jet would be proud of you."

"I just need to know if Darla is alright," Dart stopped smiling.

"Tell you what?" said Sol as he came next to Dart and threw his arm across his shoulder. "Come with us, Dart. You can't wander around the woods crying."

"Yeah," said Sal. "We have an extra room. You can stay with us." He also joined Sol and went to Dart on the log.

"I don't know," said Dart. "I miss my friends. I'll just make you miserable. Plus, I don't want to be a burden."

"No, you won't," Sol replied. "Because you made two new friends." Sol had a beaming smile on his face.

"Yeah," Sal agreed. "Plus, it isn't quite safe to be out here all by yourself. There are birds and animals of every kind out here."

"Do you mean that?" Dart asked hopefully, feeling a bit relaxed and safe. "Are you sure?"

"Yes sir," said Sal, looking around. "Besides, it'll be dark soon, and we shouldn't be out here in the dark."

"Okay," said Dart, getting up. "I guess I'm ready," he said uncertainly.

Dart and his new friends set off for Sal and Sol's house.

"You said it'll be dark soon," said Dart. "What happens when it gets dark outside?"

"There are animals in the woods," Sal replied. "And you don't want to be grabbed by any one of them, trust me!"

"We never had to worry about animals in the house," Dart answered with a sigh.

"We aren't in the human world anymore," Sal replied. "In time, you will see. And no one has ever made it back to that world. At least not that we know of. Besides, I'm tired."

"Wait," said Dart, "You get tired? I've only heard humans say that. What is that really?" he asked.

"Yeah, one of the many changes you go through to adjust here. Your body starts to feel weak, and you need to take a nap, sleep, or sit for a long while before you can work again. You will get the hang of it soon!" With that, the three started walking.

In another twenty minutes of walking, they reached a blue wooden house.

"You have your own house!?" Dart said in disbelief.

"No humans!" Sal opened the door, and they all went in. "Over here," he pointed to the left, "is the kitchen." The kitchen had a table and chairs and a pantry. "Over here," Sal pointed, "is the living room." The living room had a couch, table, two chairs, and a bookcase.

"Books?" asked Dart, "You have books here? I mean, can you read 'em too? Back home, I don't think anyone can. Maybe the elder socks, I don't know, but not everyone. This is fascinating!"

"Yeah, we do. They appear in the woods and such," replied Sal. "Anyway, here is my room," he said, pointing to a large room with beds similar to the ones the boy had back home. "And that is Sol's room." Sol's room had a telescope, which Dart was looking at and wondering, *what could a sock possibly do with that?*

"I like looking up at the sky at night," said Sol.

"And this, Dart, is your room," Sal said, directing Dart to a room that was almost similar to his own.

Dart's room had a bed, a chair, a desk, and a window. He looked out the window, and all he saw were trees. "Woah! That is a lot of trees! Thank you both again," said Dart.

"Hey! No problem," said Sal. "We are glad to have you. Anyway, it's dark, and Sol and I have to get up early. But I don't think you should be left alone tonight. Maybe we should stand watch."

"Oh no, please, it's fine," said Dart. "Just go. I don't want to cause you any kind of trouble! Thank you very much for helping me."

"It is good to have another friend," Sal replied "and remember, we are in the other rooms. Just yell if you need us." Sol closed the door.

Once alone, Dart curled up on the bed and softly cried. The faces of his friends came to his mind. Jet would buzz by here and there, followed by Marty and Meg, and then finally Darla. He closed his eyes and whispered to himself. "I am going to find my way back! For Darla and for my Friends!!"

CHAPTER 5
EAST SOCKTON

Dart woke up the next morning.

"I can't believe I became tired. I wonder why that is?"

Getting up, he felt a loud growl from his stomach.

"What?! Huh!... What just… did that come from inside?" Dart asked himself. He waited for a little to see and make sure where the growling sound came from. He bent over himself, stuck his ear to the stomach, and waited again. The growl came again, this time louder. "Woah! It really is coming from inside!" Dart said, amused and confused.

He had never felt that before. He was about to hear another rumbling sound from his tummy when there was a knock on the door.

"Who's there?" Dart asked.

"It's me, Sal!" said the voice. "Are you okay?"

Dart opened the door. "I don't know. I do have a weird feeling here, though," Dart replied, pointing to his stomach. "Looks like something has gotten inside. But how? And why didn't I notice?"

"Hehehe! That is one of the funniest explanations I have heard!" replied Sal. "That's hunger, actually, and don't worry, it's just normal. Nothing has gotten inside you! Just follow me," he laughed and patted Dart on the back.

Dart realized the growling didn't cause any pain. That relieved him a lot. Dart followed Sal to the kitchen, all the while tapping at and listening to his stomach on the way.

There sat Sol, reading. Dart was amused to see a peeled orange in front of him. Sol had one slice of the peeled orange in his mouth. Dart had seen Mom and the boy eat an orange many times before but couldn't recall any sock ever doing that, not even the elder, older ones.

"Good morning, Dart," said Sol, looking up. "How did you sleep?"

"Good," said Dart and then, after waiting for a while, added, "given that it was my first time. Even though there is something growling inside, which Sal told me is hunger. I've never really slept before, so…"

"You'll get used to it," Sol replied with a smile on his face. He looked down at Dart's hands, which were holding his stomach. He giggled and said, "Let it go; it won't run away!"

"He has a stomach growl!" Sal said. "To make the growl go away, you have to eat," he added, saying each word slowly to make sure Dart understood what he was saying. He was also acting out each and everything he was saying and giggling at Dart's confusion, but Dart didn't mind it. He had taken them to be his friends. "Help yourself," Sal said, pointing to a basket that had fresh fruits and vegetables in it.

Dart picked up a tomato, investigated it, and then swallowed it whole. He then grabbed an orange, looked it over, and started to eat it the same way. With half an orange stuffed in his mouth and the other half in his hand, he looked up. Sal and Sol were smiling.

"I-I'm sorry," said Dart, looking down, embarrassed. "I haff no inndeaa how to eeaaa thifff!" he said with a stuffed mouth.

"No, you're fine," Sal replied, swatting his hand. "We were all like that at first. You are adjusting to feeling hungry, that's all. You have to learn to chew."

"It feels weird sitting here with no humans appearing; I am used to them going around…" said Dart.

"Right on that! My friend. But you will get by just fine!" agreed and reassured Sol.

"What else will happen to me next?"

"Well, for starters, your head will fall off," Sol replied

"WHAT!" Dart exclaimed, eyes really wide and jaw dropped! The orange came flying from his mouth.

"Stop it, Sol! No one's head is falling off. Knock it off already!" said Sal, frowning.

"Dart, don't listen to him. He can be a bit of a jokester sometimes." He added, calming Dart down.

"Yeah, but you like the jokes, buddy," Sol replied.

Sal smiled. "Of course I do, but not with the new ones, remember? Just let Dart settle in, okay?"

"Deal," said Sol. He grabbed an apple from the basket, took a bite, and curled himself on the chair next to the one Sal was sitting on.

"Dart, we will be going into town today. You can see everything there." Sal invited Dart.

Dart continued eating.

"Sal," Sol began, "I don't like what I'm seeing. Turtle Pass may become a pipeline."

"We just need to tell the others," replied Sal.

"Anyway, I'm ready to leave." Getting up, Sol headed for the door. "Let's go! There is so much to show Dart," he added as he rushed towards the door.

Dart and Sal followed Sol. Going out the front door, Dart looked around.

"This is so bizarre!" he said. "Bizarre and exciting at the same time!" He looked around and marveled at everything he saw. The beautiful flowers amazed him with colors, and the animals and birds running and flying around made him giggle and excited.

They started walking down the path. A group of bunnies hopped by.

"Oh! Look at the dust bunnies!" Dart pointed excitedly.

The bunnies immediately stopped and looked at Dart.

"Uh," Sal whispered, "those are lint bunnies. We don't use the word dust here."

"Oh," said Dart. "I'm sorry. Lint bunnies!" he shouted. With that, the bunnies hopped away. "I didn't know."

Sal grinned and said. "It's okay. You will learn a lot today. Just don't call anyone anything unless we tell you what is what and who is who. Fair?"

"That'll be great!" Dart said with both of his thumbs up and pointing at Sal.

After about 10 minutes of walking, they came to a bigger road.

"Sal and Sol!" a voice called out from behind.

The three turned around. Up ran a red and blue sock.

"How are you both this morning? Looking forward to tonight?" The red and blue sock chirped excitedly. He was very happy to meet Sal and Sol.

"We sure are," Sol replied. The sock then looked at Dart.

"I'm Davet. What's your name?" he asked, smiling broadly.

"Davet," said Sal, "This is Dart. A friend of ours."

"Well, if he is a friend of yours, he is a friend of mine," smiled Davet and extended a hand to Dart.

"Thank you," replied Dart, happy to be welcomed with such enthusiasm.

"Anyway," Davet continued, "I have lots to do. See you tonight. Oh, and Dart, you are coming too, new friend!" With those words, Davet ran off.

Sal and Sol smiled.

"Davet is a good sock, Dart," said Sal and then continued, "He is always helping a sock in need. He's probably the busiest sock in the town too."

"What's tonight?" asked Dart. He was finding it difficult to hide his excitement of getting out, making new friends, and getting invited.

"A party in town," replied Sal. "It'll be fun."

With that, the three friends started walking toward town.

There, Dart saw buildings. He smiled for the first time that morning.

"This is amazing!" he exclaimed.

Sal and Sol smiled also. They were glad to see Dart cheering up.

"Welcome, Dart," Sol waved his arm, "to East Sockton!"

It was an extremely busy town. Dart was only in a few rooms his whole life. This was endless to him. There were huge, towering buildings everywhere he saw. Dart could only look around in amazement. Socks were everywhere, going in every direction. There were socks of all kinds and colors. On his left, he saw an elderly, old sock sitting on a bench in a park with a few ducks pecking around him. He would have walked to the bench when suddenly a horse cart rushed past him.

"Horses!" Dart shook his head. "How?" he asked out loud.

"I can answer that, Dart," said Sol. "In this world, there are no humans, so growth is possible. We have all sorts of animals here."

They continued walking. A sock was hammering a piece of paper on a pole. Other socks were hanging in front of a building, sharing a laugh. A group of small socks were running around laughing. And the noise! So much noise! All of a sudden, Dart felt dizzy again.

"I need to sit, I'm sorry," he said.

"No worries, sit on the curb," said Sal. "It's a lot to take in. Take all the time you need."

A few minutes passed. "Okay, I feel a little better," said Dart, slowly getting up. "I just miss not sharing this experience with the others! Oh, how I miss them," he sighed. "Especially Darla," he started to sob and wipe his eyes.

"Hey!" said a female voice. "Where were you two last night? And why is that sock crying?"

They turned around. It was an orange sock standing with her hands on her hips.

"Oh, hi, Suzy," said Sol. "This is Dart. We found him out by Turtle Pass."

Embarrassed, Dart quickly dried his eyes. "Why would you two be out by there?" Suzy asked. "You know there are throwaways in that area."

"Throwaways?" Dart asked. "There are throwaways here too?"

"Yes," Suzy replied.

"So, it makes sense," said Dart, with a faraway look in his eyes. "If lost are here, throwaways would be here too."

"Yuppers," said Sol. "But throwaways are hostile. No one knows why. High Elder reached out to some of them, but they refused to talk to her. It's their choice."

"High Elder?" asked Dart.

"Yes, she is the oldest sock in town and had enough ideas to be chosen as the ruler of our town," replied Suzy. "What's your name?"

"Oh, I'm Dart." Dart said with a sad face and then continued, "Nice to meet you. I guess I'm considered lost. In the other world, we often heard stories about the lost and throwaways but never really gave it a lot of thought. It was just a wild story."

"Well, look around," Suzy exclaimed, waving her hand. "Does 'this' look like a wild story?"

"No," said Dart. "It feels like my imagination is too wild. Maybe I'm still home."

"No," said Sol, "you are definitely in East Sockton. Anyway, stay away from Turtle Pass," said Suzy. "I have to go and attend some other business."

"Oh! Before you leave, take these papers," said Sal, handing Suzy the bundle. "It has interesting information."

Suzy took the bundle. "Thanks for these," she replied.

"It has key points," Sal said.

"Ok, well, see you later," said Suzy, walking away. "Nice to have met you, Dart," she said, looking over her shoulder with a grin.

Dart thought there was more to the grin, but he just waved and said goodbye. Sal and Sol chuckled.

"Come on, Dart," they said. "There's more to see."

Dart began walking.

Suddenly, he heard someone shout, "Move!"

Looking up, he saw a wagon close to running him over. Dart screamed but was pulled out of the way by Sal seconds before the wagon would have hit him.

"Dart, you have to remember to be more alert!" said Sal in a concerned voice.

"Sorry," said Dart. Just then, up ahead, the three friends saw a group of socks waving their arms and shouting angrily.

"Wait here, Dart!" said Sal and then told him, "Sol and I will be right back."

The two socks approached the group, and everyone started speaking in hushed tones. They talked for several minutes. Finally, Dart grew curious and walked up to the group just in time to hear Sal say, "We will discuss this with High Elder!"

Satisfied, the socks thanked him and walked away.

"Discuss what?" Dart was curious.

"Oh! Uh!" began Sal, whirling around.

"Just disagreements. Nothing to wonder about," Sol quickly chimed in, looking at Sal.

"Anyway, Dart, this is where town socks meet up. Over there," he pointed, "is our library. And over there is a hardware store."

"What is a hardware store?" Dart asked.

"It's a place where you can buy things to build with."

"Oh! Like the dad where I lived. He built things," Dart replied.

"Anyway," Sal continued, pointing, "If you go down that road, that's where you will find orchards. We get our food from there."

As Dart looked, he stepped onto the road again.

"Dart!" said Sal. "You are on the road again. You have to be careful."

Continuing the walk, Sol pointed out a tailor shop where you can get fixed, a dancing hall for socks to hang out, and lots of other places. Dart's head was spinning. The three then reached the town square. It was like in the human world. It was the main meeting place where socks gathered to discuss current events, as well as various merchants selling their goods. In the square was a tall, round building made of stone surrounded by socks. It had a clock on top of it.

A clock, Dart thought. "Sal, what's that?" Dart asked, pointing at the building.

"That is where High Elder lives," answered Sal.

"Oh, the one who runs the town?" said Dart. "I remember you saying that."

"Well, we will leave soon. Everything closes around 8 o'clock," said Sal.

"We also use the time here, Dart. Actual time. Not when humans come and go. But anyhow, why don't you sit down on that bench and look around? This is a beautiful place, friend. You will soon start liking it," said Sol. "We have to go take care of some things. We will be right back," he added.

Dart sat down and looked around. There was just so much to take in. He had to remember not to walk on roads. Then there was the time and eating and getting tired. Dart never thought he would be able to experience all that the humans did. Everything around him was lint, and goodness knows how much more there was. Sal and Sol were friendly enough, had food and all, but they weren't funny like Jet.

A couple of socks walked past. "Hello," they said.

Dart just waved half-heartedly. He couldn't feel anything but sadness. A horse carriage stopped in front of him. In the reflection, he saw him and Darla playing around in the room at night.

"One day we will get out too Darla and roam around the world!" he remembered himself saying to Darla.

"Oh, you are so brave, Dart. I will only do it if you are with me too!" Darla replied. He closed his eyes, and the faces of his friends started floating in front of his eyes.

Dart remembered all the times he told the other socks that they shouldn't be afraid of anything and then saw himself in the reflection of another carriage passing by. He looked at himself and was ashamed that he was now scared of everything. He finally thought he had had enough. His fear then turned into a determined feeling. He decided he WILL succeed here. He WILL accept this new challenge!

He looked up at the sky and then called out loud, "Darla! I miss you, but I will be the tough sock you've always seen in me."

Just then, Sal and Sol walked up and interrupted him. "Are you ready, Dart?" They asked.

"Yes, I am," Dart replied in a firm voice. He quickly collected himself and asked. "What were you looking at earlier at the house?" asked Dart.

"Oh, just maps," answered Sal. "We draw out what the area looks like. It helps others. We are mapmakers."

"Mapmakers and nap takers," said Sol in a deep voice and clicked with his teeth. They all laughed. Dart finally had to accept that this was his new home. He also decided that he would find Darla, but first, he had to sort things out for himself.

He spent his days going on walks, helping the town socks build wagons and homes, picking fruit, and hanging out with Sal, Sol, Davet, and sometimes Suzy. Suzy always made him laugh. Davet was always a help and coordinated a lot of events. He never really encountered a throwaway. No one in town ever talked about them. The days turned into weeks, then months, then finally over a year. Dart was finally part of his new world. One day, Dart was out and about.

Suzy approached him. "Dart, are we going moon-watching tonight?"

"Of course, Suzy," Dart replied.

"It'll be good to get away for a little. But right now, I must go get this fixed," he laughed, showing a small hole.

"Do you mind if I come along?" Suzy asked.

"No, not at all," replied Dart. The two started walking toward the tailor shop. Just then, a sock approached them.

"Are you Dart?" he asked.

"Yes," replied Dart.

"This is for you," the sock then said, handing him a note.

Dart opened the note and read it. He then looked up at the sock and said in a low voice, "High Elder wishes to see me?" Suzy's eyes grew wide.

"Yes," said the sock. "You are to go to the tower tomorrow at 8 am."

Dart then looked at the sock and said the obvious answer to the sock, "NO!"

Suzy and the other sock looked astonished.

"Dart, High Elder has never requested to see anyone. This is an honor." She said, trying her best to convince Dart.

"Why would she want to see me?" countered Dart. "I've been here for a while and never bothered anyone. It just seems weird. I haven't been a trouble maker, have I?"

"It is an honor," said the other sock in an orderly manner. He was an official messenger of High Elder. He fixed his stare at Dart and then said, "One that shouldn't be taken lightly."

"Just go, Dart," Suzy then said. "Do it for us, your friends? It will be fun, trust me!" She smiled.

Dart sighed. "Fine, tell her I'll be there," he told the other sock.

The sock smiled. "It's a wise choice. Oh, and not a word to anyone. Both of you."

Suzy and Dart nodded. The sock then marched off. Suzy and Dart continued to the tailor shop.

"I can't believe this," Dart mumbled. They reached the shop.

"I'll see you tonight," Suzy told Dart.

"I have to talk to my friends."

"Oh! Arma and Amawe," said Dart. "Tell them I said hi."

"Tell us what?" Dart looked back. Arma and Amawe, two purple socks (Arma was just a shade lighter), were behind them.

"Where did you two...?" Dart began, "Aah! Never mind".

Suzy laughed. "They are sneaky, Dart. Anyway, see you tonight." Suzy and the others walked off.

The next morning, Dart left the house. Sal and Sol were not home. They left the day before and were traveling to Barsock, another town five days away. Dart wouldn't see them for a few days. *Good,* he thought. *The less they know, the better.* Dart was anxious and nervous about meeting High Elder.

Soon, he was at the door of the tower. A big, bulky sock in armor pointed a staff at him and asked him to stop. The armored sock came forward, and Dart quickly fumbled in his pocket to find the note the messenger sock had given him. He handed it to the guard. The guard carefully read it, nodded, and then opened the door.

"Just start climbing the stairs," he said in a hoarse and heavy voice but with a smiling face. "Her door will have a gold and silver emblem on it. Just go right in," he added and gave a head tip to Dart.

Dart started climbing. He went past floor after floor. "She probably lives at the very top," he grumbled to himself.

On the top floor, he saw the door with the emblem to the side. He walked right in as he was told. He entered a large room. Across the room, a sock was staring out of the window silently.

"I was expecting you, Dart," she said, turning around in an orderly manner.

"Can I ask why?" Dart asked, his voice shaky.

"You have adjusted very well here. I'm glad for that," said the sock, ignoring Dart's question. The sock then approached him, holding out her hand.

"I am High Elder. And we have plans for you."

CHAPTER 6

THE HIGH ELDER'S SOCIETY

Dart was a little curious and very nervous. "A plan? For me? A... I ... I think there might be some confusion."

High Elder then smiled. She was a purple and yellow sock. Tall and lean. She walked with grace and was wearing a large pink gown with patterns all over. The gown was too long and made it look like she was floating in the air. She was visibly old but well-composed for her age. Dart instantly stopped the moment she saw her smile. He focused on her eyes, which looked tired as if the weight of the East Sockton was on her. In a way, it was, as Dart would soon find out.

"I work hard on not looking worried," she spoke as if sensing that Dart was looking at her eyes. "It is difficult because I stay very busy, but I manage." She chuckled.

"Do you know what it takes to run a town? The meetings, the decisions, plus not to mention all the events I must attend. All while being alone," she said and waved her hands gracefully at the words "meeting," "decisions," and "events." She had a smile on her face until that point, but that smile disappeared as she started the next sentence. "And now…" she began but paused and pointed out of the window, "And now I must deal with THIS. THIS growing THROWAWAY threat."

She immediately calmed herself and softened her tone. "I know some are in town. But I may be wrong about them being a THREAT…" her voice trailed off.

"But why did you want to see me?" Dart asked.

High Elder walked back to the window and looked out. She took a deep breath in and then sighed and slouched a little. Dart could sense she was tired and worried.

After a minute, she spoke, "A big confrontation may be brewing with the throwaways, Dart, and there isn't much we have prepared for it because we don't know everything yet. The throwaways have been causing us trouble for some time now, and they are growing stronger every day. They had a new leader for over a year. Their old leader, Calas, was surly too but he and I had some talks. They were brief, but I could at least bargain with him."

"Now, there is someone new. Someone more fierce and he isn't friendly. He doesn't even want to talk. I have socks gathering intel, but that won't be sufficient. I need a recruit. Someone who is friendly with the town socks. A lot of them like you. I can use that." She had turned away from the window.

"Aa… I don't… I think there is a misunderstanding… I cannot…" Dart tried to make a sentence but couldn't.

"The town needs someone who they feel comfortable with. If not for my group, I'm afraid the throwaways would overrun this town. Their mischiefs are on the rise; I don't know how long we can hold them unless we have more information," she informed Dart.

"What group?" Dart asked with intrigue and curiosity.

"This town has protection, Dart," High Elder said, "Sure, we have soldiers…" she lowered her voice and leaned a bit towards Dart and whispered, "but there are others in the shadows. Others that aren't easily noticed by the socks. And I want you to join."

"I am… I think you are misinformed," Dart said, astonished and worried.

"You were recommended by some socks." High Elder smiled and then continued, "And not just some socks, but socks I trust. Plus, by what I have seen and heard, I think you will fit quite well."

"Heard? You have heard about me? By who?" Dart was amazed.

"We have a lot of eyes and ears, Dart," she replied and sat on her chair.

"Okay. Suppose I join this 'group' of yours," said Dart, not quite trusting her. "Then what?"

"You will be trained and taught our ways. We will share with you our resources to teach you everything. There will be times when you might face danger, but we will train you how to face that too. I can promise you that there you'll be part of something grand! You will have a great purpose," replied High Elder.

"I... I don't know… I guess" Dart said.

High Elder got from her seat and walked to Dart. She placed her hand on his shoulder and said, "Don't say that, Dart! You are one of the most capable socks I have heard about. I have seen how you have adjusted so quickly."

"Okay, I guess then I will give it my best shot, and I'll join your group," he said. He was not very sure about his decision, but High Elder's words have given him confidence.

"Good!" High Elder beamed. "Come back here at 11 pm tomorrow, and we'll have things ready for you." She tapped Dart on the shoulder and got up. She turned away but immediately turned around and said strictly, "And remember! Do not tell anyone about this. Total secrecy!"

"Ok, Total secrecy!" Dart echoed and made a gesture of zipping his lips. With that, High Elder walked back to her chair.

He waved her goodbye. When he was about to leave the room, High Elder called out, "Total secrecy, Dart! Do not forget!"

The next morning, Dart woke up excited and thrilled. He had made friends in this new place, which had many other socks living happily. And now he was joining a secret organization. He wondered how he was supposed to never tell his friends. He especially wanted to tell someone else, but for some reason, he couldn't remember who. Anyway, it didn't matter. All day, he worked, stopping only to eat lunch. At 10:30, he quietly crept out of the house and walked down the road toward town. It was a moonless night. Even though he had prepared the whole day for this, he was still nervous and jittery. Aside from a few stragglers, it was mainly deserted and quite dark. Dart never liked going through town in the dark. He quickly reached the tower.

A sock with a hooded robe approached him. He looked mysterious, but Dart knew he, too, might have orders to keep things secret, and he might be a part of the secret group too. Holding up a lantern, he motioned for Dart to follow him. They reached the entrance to the tower and went inside. This time, though, the hooded figure opened a door with winding steps leading down. He nervously followed the figure down. Dart looked down the stairs and couldn't see much except for a faint flicker of fire torches lined along the stairs. Everything else was dark and damp. Dart gulped and started behind the hooded sock. After going down more than a hundred steps, they reached the bottom. There was a long passageway with a door at the end of it. It was darker than the stairs, but the hooded sock had picked a torch on the way down. Reaching the door, the figure knocked in a specific rhythm and waited. A tap was heard from the other side of the door, and then the hooded sock tapped back. This time, the door opened, and Dart entered a small, blank room with just one door.

"Wait here until that door opens, then go in," the figure said. Then he left. Dart was now in total darkness. He couldn't help but hear low-pitched music and chanting from somewhere. Finally, the door opened, and Dart walked in. The room was brightly lit. Dart squinted his eyes and then gasped. There was a long table with High Elder sitting facing him. But Dart was gasping at who else was there.

Suzy, Sal, Sol, and Davet were seated in chairs lined next to High Elder. "Greetings, Dart," said High Elder. "Sit right there, please."

"Suzy? Sal? Sol?" Dart says in a shocked voice. "H-H-How?" he stammered. Dart sat down on a chair facing them.

"Welcome," said Davet, smiling.

"So, this is the group?" asked Dart.

"Sal, Sol, and you, Suzy? Were the secrets necessary?"

"Yes, Dart," Suzy replied, "this is a serious business."

"Well, who are you in the 'group'?" Dart asked. "Who is who?"

"I am the leader," said High Elder. "Davet is my second in command. Suzy is our scout. Sal and Sol are surveyors, and Koki is the leader of our force of soldiers." She points to the empty chair. "Koki normally is there but he is on vacation currently."

"That answers a lot of my questions," Dart replied as he relaxed a bit to see the familiar faces. "But why the secrecy?"

Suzy looked at High Elder, who nodded. "Well," began Suzy, "Our town was always peaceful. Socks were working together and looking to expand. There are other places out there, but East Sockton is away from the chaos of Socktopolis. We developed our own orchards and supply stores. But then throwaways developed their own area a week away. It's the closest throwaways have been to the lost. We reached out to them in talks of trade and peace. We were getting close, but their leader, Calas, was overthrown by another. All talks stopped after that. So, we decided to form a group, which is a 'Society.' We didn't want to panic the town socks so that's why it's a secret. We hide in the shadows and stay in the background, but ALWAYS watch."

"I guess if you all are in, how can I refuse?" says Dart.

"Good," High Elder replied. "With that," she then gets up and pulls out a small staff. She walked around to the table where Dart was seated and motioned for him to rise. In a solemn voice, she then asked, "Are you prepared to defend East Sockton from any threat?"

"YES!" Dart said firmly with a beaming smile on his face.

"Do you pledge loyalty to our group?" She asked another question

"Yes," Dart replied with the same enthusiasm.

Sal and Sol then got up and approached him. "Are you able to keep this group a secret?" They asked in unison.

Again, Dart replied, "Yes."

Suzy and Davet then approach him. "Are you ready to face any danger or threat from an enemy if one becomes known to us?"

Dart replied, "Yes!"

Finally, they all ask, "Are you committed to peace?"

Dart answered, "Yes!" Each question motivated him and filled him with energy.

High Elder then smiled. "Excellent!" she said. She held out a goblet and ordered, "Now drink!"

Dart looks at the contents. It was a dark red liquid. "Oh no! Is that blood?" He yelled.

Everyone looked puzzled. Sal and Sol were disgusted. Even the music and chanting stopped.

"It's just beet juice!" Suzy mumbled incredulously.

"Yeah," said Sal, "what do you think we are? Vamp socks?" They all laughed, including Dart. Just as Dart drank, Sol leaned and whispered in Dart's ears, "We lied; it's blood,"

"Puffft! What," Dart shot the juice out of his mouth, coughing.

Sal just frowned. Sol laughed loudly. "Just kidding. Got you again, Dart."

Dart wiped his face and remarked. "I got to learn how to know when you are pulling a prank."

"Remember, no mention of our existence. Understand?"

Dart nodded. Davet then embraced him. "Welcome aboard, Dart. Well, I'm off for a lot of rest. I have a meeting with a certain someone in Argylonia," he winked.

"Ok then," said High Elder. "This concludes our meeting."

With that, everyone said good night and went their separate ways.

Sal, Sol, and Dart started walking home.

"So, you never went to Barsock. Was this your plan all along? To recruit me?" Dart asked.

"No, it wasn't," said Sol. "It was just you adjusted so well, and you get along with a lot of the town socks. It just made sense." "Plus," continued Sal, "you have a great memory. It's a useful skill." The three reached home.

Once inside, Sal yawns. "I'm tired. I'm lying down. You two have a good night."

"Goodnight, Sal," the others replied.

"Well," said Sol, "I'm beat also. See you in the morning, Dart. And congratulations."

Dart went to his room. As he closed the door, he saw Sol plop himself into the air and crash on his bed.

CHAPTER 7
THE THROWAWAY LEADER

A sock sat at a desk in a shadowy room, looking at some papers. When he didn't find what he was looking for, he called out, "CHEMI!" with his gravelly voice. He waited for a reply. When he didn't get a reply, he shouted a question, "Where are those papers I need?"

"Coming now," Chemi replied in her small voice. She was a black sock with an orange circle on it. She was Lean and smart. She walked up to the sock and handed him a pile of papers.

The tall sock grunted something that sounded like a thank you. Chemi couldn't understand what he said. She was too scared to ask again, so she just nodded her head. Backing away, she left the room quietly. The tall sock looked at one paper after another. With each paper, the smile on his face got bigger and bigger. When he was done looking at all of the papers, he smiled. He chuckled spookily and said to himself. "Finally!... Some useful information to expand my piece of the pie!" He flapped the paper in one hand and made a fist with the other. "I'm tired of a slice. I WANT THE WHOLE PIE! Hahahahaha!! And this time, I will have it!" He slammed his fist on the desks and continued laughing.

He got out of the creaking chair he was sitting in and stretched his hands. He approached the lone window in the room. There, the light hit his face. And what an evil-looking face it was! The tall sock was half white, half gray. It had small eyes that looked normal from a distance, but from closer observation, you could see that one of his eyes was droopy. He also had a permanent scowl on his face. His mouth was also a little droopy, and his stitching was crooked. It had a few scars on his chin too.

Thinking back, he remembered when the other socks whispered when he walked by. They laughed, always quietly, but he could still hear them. He pretended not to notice but it deeply hurt him. The tall sock was always treated badly. No one wanted to be his friend. Whenever he tried to make friends, the other socks would make fun of him and push him away. No one ever even returned a smile. No one talked to him except his mate, Jolene. She never judged him or mentioned his looks. She wasn't irregular. She made him laugh and smile. In fact, the only time he ever had a good time was when he was with Jolene. She never questioned, like the other socks, how they were mates. Other socks even made fun of Jolene and the tall sock being together because Jolene was beautiful and he was hideous. Jolene never thought that way, though. She loved to explore, was sociable, and made friends with everybody. She used to tell him that looks do not matter and that a sock who isn't quite smart, handsome, or beautiful can still be a good sock. That was why he loved her so much, and she loved him too. He was always cautious and protective of her.

The man of the house, where the tall sock lived before coming to East Sockton, had a female companion who would occasionally visit. She had a small dog that loved to chew things. All the socks would scream and run and hide the moment the silly dog would enter the house. Even Jolene hid. The socks were happy when the dog left.

One day, the man's friend came with a dog of his own. This dog was fast. He roamed around the house and came into the bedroom. There was chaos everywhere. Socks were running everywhere. Some socks stumbled. The dog would sniff them but move to the next. This gave the socks the chance to hide. All the socks were quietly hidden, making sure not to move at all. Suddenly, the dog saw movement to his left. He saw a sock move ever so slightly in a shoe. It was Jolene who was trying to push another pink sock further into the shoe so that the dog wouldn't see it. The dog saw her instead and quickly went and grabbed her in its jaws.

"JOOOLLLLEEEENNNNEEE!!!" The pink sock cried out loud.

"HEEELLLPPPP!!" Jolene screamed, but no sock moved except the tall sock. He grabbed a brush and smacked the dog in the face, but it only yelped and ran off with Jolene still in his mouth. He remembered her horrified eyes. Suddenly, he heard the man and his friend with the dog leaving. He was in tears. The other socks tried to comfort him, but he shrugged them away. "Why should they care now?"

A couple of days passed. He sat alone. The only sock that comforted him was gone. For the first few days, he was sad and hurt. Then he started feeling angry. "I will never be happy now!" he whispered to himself. He refused to be with the other socks. They have always loathed him. That night, he sock left through the dog door. There was heavy rain outside, but he didn't care. He just walked and walked. He didn't care if he was wet or not. He just wanted to be as far as possible from there. He walked till he could, but the rain had gotten stronger. He didn't know where to go, so he decided to seek shelter under the garbage bags next to a dumpster.

His eyes grew heavy, and he fell asleep. He awoke sometime later. The rain had stopped, but he wasn't under the bags anymore. He adjusted his eyes to the bright sun. He squinted and saw that there was no house or any dumpster around. He was on a pile of green dirt on the side of a mountain. The house was gone. There were just trees and rocks. He closed his eyes, thinking it was his imagination. He closed his eyes, waited, and then opened them again. Still, everything around him was the same. Where was he?! He slowly got up, and that was when the panic began. Slowly, he walked while yelling.

"HELLOOOO!!! ANY BODYYYY!!!!" He remembered walking for days until he found a small settlement.

That was how he met Chemi. She was a researcher sock and was studying and collecting information about this new world. Soon, Chemi took the tall sock for her companion. She taught him the ways of the new place she had learned through living out there and studying. She also taught him the difference between lost and throwaways. After spending a week at the settlement, Chemi and he set off together to a settlement in the mountains. There, he met a sock called Calas. He was the throwaway leader. He wanted to try to work with the lost. In time, he became Calas's second in command. He played the role but secretly thought Calas was weak. He started talking with other socks. He talked of his vision. He talked of glory. He got the other socks to understand his vision. They all didn't like the lost, but they listened to Calas. He was their leader, after all. Knowing he had to get rid of Calas, the sock decided to challenge Calas's role. One day, he openly challenged Calas to a fight for the leadership. A throwaway had the right to challenge at any time, but none ever did. No one wanted to lead. Calas was shocked that he challenged him. After a tough contest, Calas was defeated. He then banished Calas from the settlement. He had socks build walls around the settlement, complete with guard towers. In a year, the settlement was renamed **Warrenark**. And he was now the recognized leader. But he wasn't content. The throwaways now listen to him. They had a leader who understood how they felt after all. They wanted more, so he would give them more. He would bring a war to the lost! They will fall to him and tremble in fear. The mere mention of his name will make them scream. He will slowly take over towns, starting with East Sockton! Then Lamilee, Argylonia, and then even Socktopolis. He wouldn't rest until he conquered their world and made it his. When it was all over, there would be only one leader, and that was him. "YES!" He shouted out of the window. "SOON THE LOST WILL BOW DOWN TO ME! SOON THEY WILL BOW DOWN TO JOL!!"

CHAPTER 8
THROWAWAY TROUBLE

Nage and Gamon were two throwaways who moved to the outskirts of East Sockton on orders from Jol. Nage was green and yellow and Gamon had a faded gray and purple color. The lost looked at them suspiciously but didn't say anything.

Nage would try to give a friendly wave and a greeting to any passing socks as he did yard work.

They would go into town to get food and laugh at the little socks playing around, but the parents of the kids would take the kids away.

"Don't pay any attention to all the bad things they are calling us, Nage," Gamon instructed his friend, "Remember, we are here on a mission, and this is all part of it!"

We just want to get the information Jol asked us to get. Nage grinned and snickered. Both were hiding behind a huge tree. Nage was drawing a map of the place with his feather pan on his scroll. He had marked all the important places of East Sockton.

"Yes! We will make them our slaves! And Jol would reward us too! He will make us his favorite generals if we do this right. remember!" Gamon giggled

Actually, Jol had sent the two to spy on the lost. They needed to know if they had a militia and what the inner workings of the town were. Both of them were secretly mapping out the layout of the town. Nage was making a dangerous weapon that he would use in his invasion of East Sockton.

They disliked the lost and didn't really care what they did. But Jol was their true leader, and they didn't dare argue when he told them to move into the town and spy on its socks. While most of the socks were doubtful and suspicious of them, some socks from East Sockton had fallen for their trap. They had made friends with Nage and Gamon and shared important information with them. Within the month, the two socks managed to know that the town had roughly 40,000 socks in it and that there was a militia too, who was very powerful and strong. But they were interested in more important details. They wanted to know about the weapons, where they were stored, where the militia was, and most importantly, who the leader was of the place and where they could find him or her. That was the most important bit.

"I want to know who leads them! If you two bring that information to me, you will be my trusted generals, and if you don't, you will end up in the dungeons!" Jol had threatened them.

They didn't dare ask anyone directly, though. They were scared that the socks would be alerted, and they both would get arrested.

One day, Nage was walking down the street, getting the usual glances. He had been just a worker sock in Warrenark. When he moved up in rank, he gained Jol's trust and wanted to impress him more. He was just looking from one sock to another, learning about the buildings and names around, when he saw a sock he thought he had seen before.

What was he doing here? He thought to himself. He stopped to stare at several socks in the middle of the road further down.

"EXCUSE ME!" an older sock growled.

"Sorry, sir!" Nage said, whirling around.

The older sock was carrying a bucket with bananas in it, which slipped, and all his bananas scattered on the ground.

"See what you made me do?" the older sock called out angrily.

Quickly, the socks around stopped whatever they were doing and glanced in the direction of the loud elder. Nage paled and realized everyone was staring at him. He didn't want to make them more suspicious, so he quickly mumbled a sorry and helped the old sock pick his bananas back into the basket. He did that quickly and instantly got up, said sorry to the old sock again, and walked away with his head down. He glanced back to make sure he wasn't being followed.

But without Nage having any idea of it, he was noticed by a bigger black sock with a white stripe from his head to his feet who had seen the whole drama with the older sock. It was Koki and he was in charge of overseeing the guards and was a master of disguises and stealth. He hoped Nage didn't notice him. Koki knew Nage wasn't just any other sock but one of Jol's top scientists. Jol dealt with things mostly with his muscles and strength. Jol was not much of a thinker and wasn't very intelligent or smart. He kept all the smart socks around him. He was strong and threatened them enough to make sure they didn't dare rebel.

Koki wanted to know why Nage was in East Sockton. At first, he thought about catching Nage and questioning him directly but then quickly decided against it. He decided that monitoring Nage secretly would be the better plan, and he might learn more if he waited and spied on him. Koki had just returned from a vacation but didn't think he'd come back to a throwaway spying in his hometown, especially a genius and dangerous scientist like Nage.

Nage had carefully made his way back home. He and Gamon had been living in a small hut in a faraway part of the town where many socks didn't come or go. Gamon was in the living room writing all the things he had learned all day and all the information he had collected. He will be sending a report to Jol.

"How was the town?" he asked Nage, who looked a little terrified.

"The usual glances," Nage answered and sighed and jumped onto the sofa.

"That's good," replied Gamon. "We will have to stay on guard. We can't let anyone know about what we are doing. I don't know about you, but I don't want to be thrown into the dungeon!" he added, shivering at the idea.

"Me neither! I made sure no one saw me coming here either," Nage replied, sounding confident. He rested for a while, passed his scrolls to Gamon, and then went to his room. Gamon continued to write and finalize his weapon design. He remembered what Jol had asked from them for the weapon he wanted to be made.

Jol wanted a weapon so horrible that the lost would tremble in fear of just the thought of it. He had worked for two weeks on the idea he had. He even built a small version of it.

"This will keep Jol quiet for now," he mumbled to himself with a wide smile on his face. They still had more research to do about the town, but at least this project was done. They had to send a report to Jol tomorrow evening. Feeling satisfied, he called Nage. The design was drawn, and the prototype was built. Nage looked at the papers and smiled. Grabbing two oranges, he tossed one to Gamon. Both of them started to laugh.

"Excellent work, Gamon. Jol would love it!" he congratulated his friend. Meanwhile, Koki needed a plan. He will go to High Elder and tell her what he saw.

He reached the tower later that day. He approached the door. One of the guards recognized him, gave a nod, and then opened the door. He walked up the long staircase.

"Koki! How are you? How was your vacation?" asked High Elder when he entered the room.

Koki saluted. "It was good. And needed," he quickly replied.

The High Elder smiled. "Well, so are you back at work? Much needed, indeed. You missed a meeting so let me fill you what you have missed. We brought in a new sock. His name is Dart."

"Dart?" said Koki, a little doubtful, and then confirmed, "The sock that hangs with Sal and Sol?"

"Yes," High Elder replied. "Suzy is working out by Turtle Pass, and Davet is on vacation in Argylonia."

Davet and Koki weren't good friends. Davet didn't hide that he didn't trust a throwaway to have so much responsibility. It bothered him. But High Elder and the rest of the group liked and trusted Koki. And to him, that's all that mattered.

"I, too, have news," Koki replied to High Elder, who was waiting for him to speak up. High Elder always knew that Koki was hardworking and would always have news about security and about the town that was important. "I've seen a throwaway in town."

"Yes, I know," High Elder replied.

"Do you know who he is?" Koki asked, sounding concerned

"No, I do not," replied High Elder.

"His name is Nage, and he is one of Jol's top minds," Koki said.

"Top mind? Oh no! Does that mean what I think it means?" said High Elder, getting out of her chair and putting her hand up to her mouth. "Whatever shall we do?" She asked as she wiped some sweat off her forehead.

"I think I should keep an eye on him. See what he is up to," Koki said with a calming tone.

Nodding, High Elder agreed. "What do you intend to do?"

"I have someone that could find info on him. I need an address," he replied.

"Alright. Keep me informed, and do what you have to do quickly. I cannot have Jol's top minds in my town roaming about freely. They definitely are up to something. We already have had trouble as it is…" said High Elder with a commanding tone. "You may go."

Saluting again, Koki whirled and left the room.

"Hopefully, he doesn't find anything wrong," she mumbled.

Koki finally arrived at his house. *It is good to be back*, he thought. He noticed his neighbor outside. He waved, but the neighbor didn't return the wave. He just went inside. Koki sighed and drooped his head. Even though he was used to such behavior from the town socks, it still hurt. He was an honest and hardworking sock and did a fine job of protecting East Sockton, but some of the lost still didn't accept him. Entering his two-room house, he collapsed on his couch. The living room contained a couch, a chair, and workout equipment. On a nearby table, there was a fighting staff and some masks. Koki, a seasoned warrior, stretched out, deciding he would do his work in the morning. After that, he planned to visit Sal and Sol and maybe even talk to Dart.

The next morning, Koki woke and hurriedly did his morning workout. He had a lot to do that day and not a lot of time. He had to find out about Nage. Koki went to a sock he knew from his spy network who could find out anything. His name was Deke. Deke had his fingers in everything and anything. You could ask Deke anything about what was going on in the town, and he would always have a nugget of information to share. Was Deke sneaky? Yes. Could he be trusted? Maybe. One thing was for sure, which was that Deke owed Koki. When Deke was in trouble, Koki had helped him by asking High Elder to spare him because he was a wealth of knowledge. Deke pledged to give Koki info whenever he needed it. So, he became Koki's eyes and ears.

Koki walked to a small house with covered windows. It was a worn-down house in a worn-down area of town. Three yellow and red socks were hanging outside. When Koki approached, they stepped in front of him.

"Where do you think you're going?" one of the socks asked.

"Just inside to talk with Deke," replied Koki.

"Well, no one sees Deke unless we say they can. And you have to pay to see Deke," the sock answered.

Rolling his eyes, Koki replies, "Look! I don't have much time. Step aside."

The sock reached out and grabbed Koki by the chest.

"Look!" he began, but that was as far as he got, and the other one of the yellow socks pushed him a little. Grabbing his hand, Koki whirled around and twisted the sock's arm behind its back.

"Ow! Let go," the sock bellowed.

The other socks slowly came toward him.

"Uh, Uh," smiled Koki. "Don't even think about it. Because if you don't let me talk to Deke after I'm through with him, it'll be worse for you two. I am his friend. Ask him. He would tell you."

"Wow!" a voice just then said from the porch. "Do you really have to treat my guys that rough?"

Koki looked over. There was a splotchy brown and white sock on the porch. It was Deke. Koki pushed the sock away from him.

Deke then looked at the others. "This sock can come and go as he pleases. Understand?"

"Yeah," they grumbled. The one sock just eyed Koki coldly while rubbing its arm.

"You did good challenging him, though," said Deke, patting the sock on the back.

"Koki, let's go inside before you break one of them into two." Koki followed Deke, smiling.

"How can I help you?" Deke then asks.

"You seem like you are doing well for yourself," Koki smiled, looking around and laughing.

"Well, I manage," Deke answered with a wink.

Deke grabbed some grapes and popped one in his mouth. "There are throwaways in town, Deke. I followed one yesterday, and there is something big that he was up to. Something terrible, I can feel it. I need to know as much as I can on him and everyone else if there are more without them knowing."

Deke slowly chewed the grape. "There are actually two."

"Seriously?" Koki sounded alarmed.

"Yup," said Deke. "Do you need some... ahem... backup?" he asked.

"I don't know. I'm just keeping tabs as of now. If I was looking for muscle, I might let you know," answered Koki. "Besides, who would be the backup? Those three outside?" Koki chuckled.

"I can do that for you," said Deke. "Now, how about you tell me about your trip? You were gone for a while."

Koki got up and smiled. "Maybe next time, Deke. Thank you for this. A lot is going outside, and I have to know what!"

Deke smiled back. "Hey, it's the least I can do, Koki. You always make sure I'm left alone."

Koki walks out the door. "I'll be waiting for the info," he says over his shoulder. "Take care,"

As Koki went down the steps past the other socks, the one sock who Koki roughed up, said, "See you again."

"I can't wait," Koki replied without looking back. It was getting late. Koki decided to talk to Sal and Sol in the morning. And, plus, he was curious about the one called Dart.

CHAPTER 9
KOKI'S MISSION

The next morning, Koki woke up to a knock on the door. Yawning, he got up to answer it. A sock was outside, and he handed him an envelope. It had his name on it. Before he could say anything, the sock nodded and took off. Koki opened the envelope and smiled; it had the information he needed from Deke. Koki smiled wider. He would have to do something nice for Deke to show his appreciation. A paper inside had the names of two throwaways: Nage and a sock called Gamon. The first one, he knew already, but he was glad he had one more name. There were some crumbled papers with markings of the town like a map. There was an address too. This was perfect. He started getting ready to meet the high Elder.

He arrived at the tower shortly after. Upon entering the room, he saw Suzy. She hugged him.

"I'm glad you are back. How was your vacation?" she exclaimed.

"Everything was great!" He quickly replied.

"Well, details later, but right now, let's talk work. It is urgent. Sal and Sol had some information on Turtle Pass. There were a few throwaways there," she reported, and he listened mindfully.

The High Elder smiled. "Do you know anything more about this "top" mind of Jol, Koki?"

"Not yet," he replied. "But I have an address and found out the name of another sock with him. I had my suspicions, and I am afraid something bigger is going on. I will get to work on this right away."

The High Elder then said the words Koki dreaded. "Take someone with you," she said.

"I prefer to work alone," he replied.

"I know Koki, but we have to see if Dart can handle himself." She insisted on Koki.

She knew Koki didn't like company – Mostly because the other socks wouldn't take to him with an open heart and mind. But matters were tense.

"The new sock?" Koki was uncomfortable. "What if he gets us caught or gives away my disguise?" He was clearly worried and wasn't confident of the plan.

The High Elder smiled and assured him, "He may be better than you think. Have him be a lookout or something."

"Yes, High Elder. But can I ask him to let me take the lead and do what I ask him to, nothing extra?" Koki asked.

High Elder nodded in agreement.

Suzy then grinned and said, "I think Dart will surprise you."

"I doubt it, Suzy," replied Koki. "But I will look forward to it. It's about time I go meet this Dart." He saluted High Elder, shook Suzy's hand, and left.

Koki arrived at Sal and Sol's house around 10 a.m. It was already sunny out. Something crashed inside. But Koki knew it would be Sol doing something silly like he used to. Koki knew Sol was a fun guy, always up to some mischief, and was one of the few socks that always welcomed Koki.

He knocked on the door.

"I'm coming; please don't break the door. Sol already has done that twice." Sal called as he opened the door with a smile. The smile widened when he saw Koki on the other side of the day. He instantly called out, "Sol, guess who's here? It's Koki." He went out and hugged Koki hard.

"Koki?" said Sol, coming from the living room with a half-bitten apple in his hand and the other half stuffed in his mouth. "How was your trip?" he asked, apple flying everywhere.

Koki smiled. "Everyone wants to know. All in due time," he replied. And without a pause added, "I'm here though to see… Dart, I guess, is what his name is, right?"

"Oh yes, Dart, you'll love him. He is a jolly fellow, but you'll have to wait. He is asleep at the moment. He had a bad night," Sal informed him, inviting Koki to point him in the direction of the living room. "I'll go wake him. You know where the living room is, right?"

Koki smiled, "Sure do!" and went to the sofa in the living room.

About two minutes later, Dart walked out. His eyes were heavy, and his mind was a little groggy.

"This is Koki, Dart," informed Sal, pointing in his direction.

"Hi, Dart!" Koki said, getting up to shake his hand.

"Koki?" Dart replied, taking his hand. The handshake was strong, and it shook Dart wide awake. "I've heard of you. You are some kind of guard."

"I'm a little more than that, Dart. Anyway, High Elder wants you to assist me." He informed Dart.

"Assist you in what?" replied Dart.

"Well," Koki began, "I have some spy work, and I need a lookout. There are two throwaways named Nage and Gamon. Have you been a spy before?"

"That is good news, Dart," said Sol. "The High Elder has faith in you. Koki usually works alone. So, this is a rare occasion. Give it your best. Koki is pretty good at spying. Second only to Suzy and her two friends, Arma and Amawe."

"I hope I live up to it," Dart said nervously.

"You will – if you do exactly what I said. Let me take charge. Would that work for you?" Koki asked, looking sternly at Dart.

"I guess so…" Dart agreed.

"Well then, let's get to work, shall we." Koki got up from the sofa, and out the two went.

"So," said Koki, walking down the path. "The High Elder seems to have a lot of faith in you. As does Suzy. So, we will see if they are right. You were given an opportunity to join our group after all."

"I felt I wasn't GIVEN a choice, but yes, I am equally glad and privileged. A little nervous too," Dart replied.

"Regardless," replied Koki immediately, "You took the oath. And now I need you to focus. There's some unrest in East Sockton, and we need to investigate it. There are some throwaways in town. Normally, that's bad enough, but one particular throwaway is one of Jol's main guys. I am worried about him the most. And there is another one with him, and they are up to something. Something disastrous. I don't know what exactly, but there is something for sure. So, we have to do some spying. I'm curious about why these two are here."

Dart just listened and followed Koki. In some time, they reached the outskirts of town. Most of the houses and buildings were boarded up, and the streets were dirty — exactly opposite to how the main area of East Sockton was. Some stragglers walked by, eyeing Koki and Dart. They looked at them with suspicion. Dart was nervous by the gazes and found it difficult to maintain focus. Koki, on the other hand, was moving without even glancing at any of them. Somewhere in the distance, a lint dog was barking. Koki looked at a piece of paper.

"There," he pointed, "that is the building, Dart."

Dart looked at the building. "It's the worst building on the block," he concluded. "So, what do we do now?" Dart asked.

"We wait and watch. And we make sure no one sees us," replied Koki.

Koki slipped behind a dumpster and waited for Dart to follow.

"What?" Dart asked.

"Get behind!" Koki whispered and directed with his head.

"There? Of all the places, a dumpster, don't we have another place in this whole area to hide?"

"This is where we are least expected to be seen. Hide before someone sees us. You can ask me all the questions from here," Koki exclaimed but made sure his voice was down to a whisper.

Dart reluctantly got behind, and the two socks hid behind a dumpster. Koki was used to this kind of work but not Dart. He disliked every minute of it. He was supposed to meet Suzy, but now that plan was crushed. Now he was with some sock named Koki behind a dumpster.

"You seem really intense on this, Koki," Dart remarked.

Koki whirled around. "Let me explain something, Dart. I am the leader of High Elder's army. And I'm a throwaway."

Dart wasn't expecting that. He gasped, "A throwaway!? Throwaways hate the lost, don't they?"

"They do Dart, but they can change. I did, after all. Some time ago, I appeared in the far north mountains. I was scared and alone. I don't know where exactly but my mate was gone. I wandered for I don't know how many days, even maybe weeks. That's when Jol found me. He brought me to where his compound was. He taught me how this world was. He and Chemi. He had hatred for the lost like I haven't seen in my life. And for a while, because of him being my mentor, I did too. But, over time, I realized that I didn't have a good reason to hate. There was nothing the lost were doing that might deserve hate. Also, I realized that I wasn't getting any fun out of it. I was angry most of the time, just like Jol. Hate isn't good. Then I noticed Jol was preparing the others for a war with the lost. I wanted to try to form a truce with the lost and live peacefully together. When I told Jol that idea, he accused me of betraying him. Then he said he had to teach me a lesson. Some of his loyal followers attacked and beat me badly and knocked me unconscious. When I came to the town, I was on a path away from the compound. So, I left and approached the lost. Naturally, they were suspicious, but I earned the trust of some of them. I worked hard to earn the trust of High Elder too. Even now, some socks look at me funny. I'm not completely trusted."

With that, the two grew silent and waited. They heard someone approach, or so the two thought. Dart was surprised to hear what he had just heard. *Someone from the other side, working for High Elder, isn't that something? This really is a funny place,* Dart thought.

"How long are we going to…" Dart was about to ask when it would be a good time to leave when he heard a horse carriage approach. He peeked from behind the dumpster and saw a lint horse stop not too far from them, towing a wagon. Two socks then came out to greet the driver.

"That's Nage," Koki whispered, pointing to one of them. "The other sock must be Gamon. These are the two I've been talking about. He is one of the most dangerous socks I know. He is a genius. The other one must be equally important too if he is with Nage," he added.

Nage and Gamon went into the building and came out carrying a crate. Looking around, they hurriedly put the crate in the back. Waving bye to the driver, they went inside. The driver started down the road, leaving town. Koki wished he could see in the crate.

"Okay, now what?" Dart asked excitedly. "It's getting dark."

"We have to get inside Dart and look around," Koki replied. "Hopefully, they leave soon."

Dart gave him a thumbs-up, making sure he stayed hidden. So far, Koki was pleased with the way Dart was working.

The two socks waited some more. The sun was finally over the horizon, and the stars shone in the night sky. Luck was with them because, after a while, they saw Nage and Gamon leaving. They started walking toward the center of town. Koki waited until they were out of sight.

"Come on, Dart, let's hurry. And put this on," said Koki, pulling out a mask.

Dart put it on, as did Koki. Looking around, they ran from behind the dumpster and crossed the street to the back door of the building.

"Cover me, Dart," said Koki, pulling out a wire. "I'm going to pick the lock. See that no one is coming or watching."

"Why don't you try the knob first? Have you given that a try?" said Dart.

Koki rolled his eyes. "Seriously, they are two outlaws, one of them a genius, and you think they would leave the door op…"

Dart twisted the doorknob, and the door creaked open

Koki looked at Dart. "Not a word," he growled and dashed in on his tiptoes.

Dart followed him, smiling. They were in the living room.

"What are we looking for, Koki?" Dart whispered.

"Anything that shows what they may be up to, plans, charts, maps, messages, scrolls… whatever we can find and use to make a link…" replied Koki.

They start looking around the couch, under the tables, and on the shelves. Finding nothing, Koki says, "Go search that room, and I'll search the other."

Dart nodded without wasting a minute. He was thrilled and excited but also very nervous. He quickly looked through the room and, when he found nothing, went to the other bedroom. There was a bed that had a sheet a little longer than the ones in the rest of the bedrooms. Both of them searched the rooms, and when they found nothing, they came together to discuss it.

"Found anything?" Koki asked

"Nope, not a thing," Dart replied.

"Think Dart, there has to be something. If Nage was here, he surely would have worked out something." Koki instructed and started thinking himself.

Where would I hide something important, or maybe where would I hide myself if that boy was coming to grab me on laundry day? he thought to himself. *Wait, I got it. It is worth a try!* He quickly dashed to the room he had just been to.

"What?" Koki asked, but Dart was in a rush.

He quickly bent down and pushed the bed a little, and voila!

Some papers were sticking out from under the bed. It seemed that someone had tried to hide them. He pulls them out and looks through them. A wide smile pressed on his face.

"This might be interesting," said Dart. He runs to the room Koki is in. Koki looked through them really quickly.

"They might be useful, Dart. Good job. This might be exactly what we might be looking for. Or at least something we can use!

Let's get out of here. We might come later, but I guess we should leave now before the two return!"

Just then, they hear the front door opening and muffled voices discussing something. It sounded urgent, and the two voices were whispering.

"We have to speed up. We must complete building the weapon before Jol sends someone for us! We have to show him something." One voice said. It sounded scared.

"I am doing as best as I can. We also have to complete making the map of this area. We haven't yet learned what we were here for," the other replied, clearly afraid.

 Closing the bedroom door, Koki and Dart ran to the window. Dart couldn't get it to open.

"Let me try, Dart." Koki strains with all his might, and the window opens. "Quick! Climb through!" he commanded Dart.

Dart climbed through, and Koki followed, making sure he did it in a hurry and did not make a noise. He was almost out when his head bumped against the window, which made it creak slightly. No sooner than Koki gets through the window, the door opens, and Nage comes into the room, listening for the faint creaking sound.

"Hello," he called out, "Is anyone here?"

Koki hid just below the window and had Dart pulled to the ground too. "Sssh!" he whispered as both of them waited for Nage to leave.

Nage took two steps in the direction of the window when Gamon yelled from the other room, "Hey, Nage! Fancy a sandwich? I am fixing myself one!"

Nage looked at the window for a while, wanting to investigate, when Gamon yelled again.

"Nage! Sandwich?!"

Nage grunted and decided the window might just be creaking because of the howling wind. "Yes! Make it two for me," he yelled and went out of the room.

Koki lifted his neck carefully to see if Nage had left the room. He had. He took a sigh of relief, and so did Dart. They darted quietly before any other adventure happened.

CHAPTER 10
A CHILLING DISCOVERY

Dart and Koki run for a few blocks. Koki looked back every so often to ensure they weren't followed. "Okay… I… I… think we are… far enough, Huff!" Koki said, panting when they had run quite a bit.

"I was…huff! Huff! Thinking the… same thing!" Dart said. He had his hands on his knees and was bent down to catch his breath.

Dart was still breathing heavily, but Koki recovered quickly.

"You should exercise more often, you know!" Koki said.

"Yes, I should!" Dart replied, still panting. Dart understood that if he had to work as a spy, he would have to be physically fit and exercise more. When both were finally calm and ready, they brought out the papers they had grabbed from Nage's house.

"What do you make of them?" Dart asked, looking curiously at the papers. He kept shuffling with the papers. He would hold it to light, or he would flip it to try and understand what the drawings on the papers meant.

"I'm not sure. I don't think I have seen anything like this before in my life. I am only sure that whatever it is, if Nage and that other genius were working on this, I am sure it is something dangerous and destructive. And we will have to figure it out soon before they do some real damage!" said Koki, alarmed. He, too, was looking carefully at the pictures. He tried harder flipping the pictures every now and then but couldn't understand what it was. He finally gave up and decided, "We have to bring them to Sal. He may know."

"That's a good idea," said Dart. "If it is as dangerous as you say it is, it is better that we hurry rather than waste time to figure it out ourselves."

Koki nodded. "Agreed. Let's get going," he said and started rolling the papers. "And..." he said and paused for a second, "I'm sorry I doubted you. You really came through tonight. This night didn't go to waste, all because of you. You helped find important information. And I don't know many socks who can keep their calm when in a tough situation like this, but you were solid enough and didn't make a dumb move in a dangerous situation. That's quite impressive."

"Oh, thank you, Koki! Means a lot! Plus, I knew you were the best of the best. The team talks about you quite highly. I knew you'd have a plan if we got into a sticky situation. And I'm sorry for the way I acted towards you, Koki. It's just that so much is happening so quickly. I am not sure who likes who and who trusts who in East Sockton. I am still getting used to everything. I hope you can pardon me for my behavior earlier!" Dart replied in a respectful manner, extending a hand.

Koki quickly took his hand and shook it firmly and strongly. Dart's whole body jittered on the handshake, but he didn't mind it.

He was happy that Koki had accepted him, and now the two were finally on good terms.

"No worries, it's all good! You'll figure out everything soon," Koki replied.

With things now sorted between the two, they darted to look for Sal. They entered the house after Koki had looked around to see no one else was watching them. Dart did the same, but he didn't know exactly where to look or who to look for. He just did what Koki did to learn from him. They entered and found Sal and Sol in the living room. Sal was attentively reading a book while Sol was skipping and counting.

"135, 136, 137… Hello spies!" he chirped when Dart and Koki

"Dart, Koki, how did it go?" asked Sal, lifting his head from the book.

"Really good, actually," Koki replied. "Dart found these papers, which surely have some important information we cannot quite make anything out of! That's what we are here for. For you to have a look at them and see if you know what they are or any other information!" He handed the papers to Sal.

Sal took the papers, unrolled them, and examined them carefully. Sol had stopped skipping and sneakily walked behind Sal. He peeked at what was on the paper.

Sal shrugged and replied while still looking at the papers, "I don't know what this is, but tomorrow is another day. Did you guys run into any problems?"

"No, we were fine," Koki smiled. "In and out."

"Yup! Can't wait to get out there again!" Dart chuckled.

"Well, on that note, I'll be taking my leave," said Koki. "I'll see you all soon." Waving goodbye, he walks out the door.

"Well, what did you think about Koki?" asked Sol.

"What do you mean?" Dart replied.

"Well, Koki always works alone. It's rare to have him take anyone," answered Sal.

"He was okay," Dart replied. "He told me how he was a throwaway and how he is still distrusted by socks, which was a little surprising for me, and I might have accidentally judged him for that but I apologised."

"That will probably last a long time," said Sal, and then added, "For a while, Sol and I didn't trust him either. But the way he had dedicated his services to East Sockton is remarkable. We can't thank him enough!"

"And also, the job went well, which gave us the chance to make things good between us. And you were right about him. He really is the best of the best. His method of doing things is perfect, almost flawless. He was like a ghost. Took me in and out without creating a ripple! It was exciting to work with him," Dart added, agreeing with Sal.

"That sounds great. I guess I should be heading to bed. I'll see you in the morning." With that, Sal goes to his room and closes the door.

Dart looked over to Sol, who was curiously and attentively looking at the papers, flipping them and holding them to the light. When nothing worked, he kept the paper down, made a fist, and peeked at the papers through the hole like a telescope. Then, he decided to use his hands as a frame to see if something made sense. Dart chuckled silently. *What funny character!* He thought to himself.

"That Nage and Gamon seem to be up to something," Sol remarked after failing to see anything that he could understand. "And we'll have to figure this out before they wreak havoc in East Sockton. I'll take these papers to the engineers tomorrow. I am sure those gearheads would understand what this is all about, of course, right after seeing High Elder with this info."

"Sounds good," replied Dart. "I, too, should go to bed. It's been a long day, and I am sure tomorrow will be similar. Must take my rest!" he said as he got up and went to the room. He waited for a witty remark that Sol usually gave, but when he didn't. Dart turned around to see Sol still shuffling the papers, trying to make out what was drawn in the papers. Sol had his face almost on the desk with the papers, one eye closed, and a magnifying glass held in front of the other. *Funniest sock out there for sure*, Dart thought and closed the door.

The next morning, Sol planned on heading to the Town Hall. First, though, he had to report to the High elder and show her the plans. The day was unusually sunny. Upon reaching the tower, he looked around. No one seemed to be watching him. Sol shook his head. Now was not the time to be nervous. He nods to a guard who lets him into the tower. Once inside, he went up the stairs and knocked on High Elder's door.

"Sol, come in. I was expecting an update on the things out there!" she said with a smile, but her smile faded when she saw the look on Sol's face. "What is it, Sol? You seem…"

Before she could complete her sentences, Sol held the papers up. "Dart and Koki found some papers in Nage and Gamon's home. I am not… WE are not sure what this is. Not Sal, not Dart, not even Koki has an idea what this is. I am going to have them checked out at town hall."

"What do YOU think the papers are?" High Elder asked.

Sol shook his head. "I can't make anything out of them. A wild guess would say this is some kind of a weapon. At least, if Nage is involved, we must at least consider that an option. It may just be nothing. I was going to bring them to the engineers."

The High Elder nodded her head. She seemed nervous and scared at Sol mentioning the weapon. She was scared if the news spread, there would be terror among the socks and if there was really a weapon.

"Go via the safe house," she instructed. "I don't want you to risk being seen with the papers outside. Just in case."

"Yes, Ma'am," said Sol. With that, Sol whirled around and left the room. The safe house was smartly built by High Elder and the team to stay hidden in plain sight. It was made on the same route that led to Sol's home, but the entrance was under the overhead bridge behind a bush. It was also built behind a chocolate and ice cream shop, so no one would suspect anything. It had a reinforced structure that was built in the last year to keep it safe from attacks. The High Elder wanted one just in case anything happened with the throwaways.

The safe house was a place to create a strategy or just to nonchalantly meet. It also had a secret entrance that went directly to the town hall. Sol reached a big clump of bushes about a block from the safe house. Looking around, he quickly ducked into the bushes. There was a door in the ground. He opened the door and walked down some stairs into a tunnel. It was one of 4 entrances into the safe house. Before, he used to think that it was tiring to take this route through the safe house as it was long and secretive, but now, with a possible throwaway threat, he was actually glad it was done. Aside from several chosen guards, only the order knew it really existed. He walked down the tunnel to a door.

Knock, Knock, Knock... Knock, Knock, Knock... Knock, Knock!

He was glad he still remembered the knocking pattern. The door opened, and an athletic-looking sock faced him on the other side. Her name was Garta.

"Hello Sol, no funny comments today, big guy? What brings you by? Everything okay. You look like you have some troubling news?" she smiled. She was lean and tall, almost as tall as the door.

"Garta! Good to see you," Sol smiled back. "Nothing that we are sure of, Garta, but yes, everything is good so far. There are some secrets we have discovered that we are investigating, but we have to be alert now!"

"Oh! That doesn't sound good," she answered, worried.

"Oh, nothing to worry about yet. Relax." Sol comforted her and smiled his usual smile.

Garta was relieved to see him smile and sighed. She was a loyal sock, respected by everyone, including High Elder. High Elder trusted her so much that she was the youngest one to join her personal Guard Corps. One of the reasons was that she was led, tutored, and mentored by Koki. She was a good student and a brave warrior. She followed every order to the letter. She was even rumored to take over for Koki if he ever stepped down.

But Sol was too nervous and scared now after he had discovered the papers with the weird drawings. He couldn't help but wonder what the future might hold. This possible throwaway threat certainly made him think about Koki. *Was Koki capable of rejoining the throwaways?* Sol shook the thoughts away. Now was not the time to be paranoid. These papers may not even be important.

"Oh, Sol," began Greta. "Did you hear about the big event Davet is planning for all the kids?"

"No," Sol replied. "Whatever it is, I'm sure it'll be good. Davet definitely is good for morale," he smiled.

"Yeah, I think he's awesome," replied Greta. "Well, anyway, I'll see you around Garta," said Sol, walking away. Sol then goes up another flight of steps and into the safe house.

The interior of the safe house consisted of six rooms along a hallway. One room was The Weapon Room, which was complete with clubs, shields, and rock slings. Koki designed it. He insisted it would be vital. Plus, he knew the throwaways better than anyone. Another room was where High Elder stayed. A smaller room right next to her was where Suzy and her two scouts, Arma and Amawe, stayed. Just across from Suzy's room was a room that Davet stayed in. One room housed Koki, Sal, Sol, and Dart. One room was for holding prisoners if such a time came. The safe house was built close to the town hall where the engineers worked. To get to the secret entrance that led to the town hall, you had to go down another flight of stairs and go down another hallway through another door. The door secretly opened into the back of a small closet that opened into a hallway. Sol opened the door slowly and peeked out. He looked left and right to make sure the coast was clear. He quickly tiptoed out of the closet and closed the door at a snail-pace, making sure it did not sound. Once he made sure the door was perfectly closed, he jogged out of the hall and into a large room at the end of the hall behind a door that stretched from wall to floor. He was finally in the engineering room.

A sock with thick glasses and ruffled and pulled threads near the ears sat at a long desk. There were all kinds of tools on the table, and he was stretching a band that was attached to a stick.

"Hey, Harf!". Harf was the town's Chief Engineer. He was one of the first socks that Sol met when he arrived in this world and was among the oldest ones in East Sockton. He was a genius and was the innovator behind most of the things in the town. They had become fairly close friends since he had helped Sol understand and learn everything. He overlooked the work of eight others. It was him that Sol wanted to see.

"Harf! You lazy bum, you would have knocked me good!" laughed Sol. "How are you?"

Harf stood up. "Whatever, Sol! I am just working on this new elastic band for the slings. I hear we need to reinforce. Got orders from High Elder!" He exclaimed, smiling, "Try being in my place for five... no, 4 minutes! You'll be a pile of tears and won't be asking this question." The two shake hands. "So, what brings you here?" he asked asked.

Sol holds up the plans. "This. Whatever this is. These were found in a home where some throwaways live and just some throwaways. Word has it that they are the two most dangerous of the lot," he replied, sounding serious. "We need to know what kind of plans these are. The papers are all mixed up, and there seems to be a small drawing on each one. I am scared it is something dreadful, but what do I know about these small drawings anyway?"

"Interesting," replied Harf. His eyes were fixed on the drawings on the plans. "I will get right on these. Anyway, how have you been?"

Sol shook his head. "This whole throwaway trouble has me up late, Harf. I haven't had a decent night's sleep in two weeks!"

Harf smiled sympathetically. "I'm sure this…" he held the plan up, "is nothing. These plans may not even be anything special. Try to get some rest while I figure this out."

Sol grinned, sighed, and sadly said, "Looks like I'll get to rest only I'm retired from this life," he said. "Maybe I'll just travel to the Far North mountains. Do you have any skis I can borrow?"

"You'll be back within a day with a broken leg, I tell you. Or you will be frozen, whichever happens first," laughed Harf.

Sol gave him a light jab on his shoulders.

"Yeah, who am I kidding? Me and the outdoors! Anyway, I am headed into town. I have to meet with some others."

"Hey Sol, we have to get together soon and have a drink. It's been a while. Me, you, and Davet. Like old times," said Harf.

"We will. I promise, once this throwaway mess settles, but only if you promise me to bring that cake you bake!" replied Sol and started to make his way towards the door.

"Cake and drinks? Can wait! Seeing you out there soon, friend," Harf waved as Sol went out the door.

Sol waved his hand with his back to Harf and was gone as the giant door closed with a thud.

Sol made sure he was quick to get out and quickly snuck into the closet before anyone could see him. He slid the back door of the closet and went all the way back to the safe house. He reached the safe house, closed the last door, and just as he turned, he was shook to see Suzy.

"Jee! Suzy, you almost gave me a heart attack! What's going on? Since when did you start wandering into the safe house?" he asked as he closed the door quietly.

Suzy shook her head. "Relax, I was looking for you. There is some activity on the outskirts. The throwaways have set up a camp about 20 miles from town," she exclaimed. "With the exception of those already in town, they've never been this close before. I wanted your opinion about sending out Arma and Amawe to look it over. Gather information and report back without being seen, you know. They got skills we can use, we need to find out what is going on before it is too late."

"Excellent idea, Su. We have to gather as much info as we can." Sol replied. "They are more than suited for the task. They are sneaky; those little ones will be in and out before the throwaways would know it. We would need High Elder's permission, though. Engaging the throwaways, even secretly, can be risky business!"

"Aye, aye. On it, then. Plus what is the deal with these papers I hear you have found? It has stirred up quite a buzz; everyone on the team is talking about them," Suzy asked curiously.

"Hush! Let's not talk about that everywhere. No one has any idea what they are. And I didn't find them. Dart and Koki did. I just dropped the papers to Harf. Maybe he would shake his brain a little and figure it out." Sol said, whispering.

"Great. I am sure that old genius will know." She said.

"I hope so!" Sol crossed his fingers.

He saw Suzy in deep thought.

"Do you think I'm overreacting about the throwaways?" she asked after a little pause.

"Oh, absolutely not. It's better to be safe than sorry," replied Sol. "Just make sure your scouts have a full report written down."

Suzy nodded. "I'm going into town to get something to drink. Care to join me?" she asked.

"It's rather early, but why not?" replied Sol. Together, the two leave the safe house. Nodding goodbye to Garta, the two leave for town.

Once in town, Sol and Suzy go to the Silver Sock to get a drink. Sol orders two beet juices with mango, his favorite. He gives one to Suzy. They just sat back and watched a band play a lively tune. It consisted of three older socks playing with metal cans and cups.

"This turned out to be a peaceful night after all," Sol remarked.

"Yeah," Suzy agreed. "Tomorrow, Dart and I are going on a nature hike."

Sol chuckled.

"Why are you chuckling," Suzy asked.

"Oh, nothing," he replied. "It just seems you and Dart have been spending a lot of time together. That's all."

Suzy turned red. "Oh, we only do it because we are coming up with a strategy," she quickly replied.

Sol smiled. "Ooh strategy! Isn't that exciting?" He was batting his eyelashes and grinning.

"Yes, we are trying to figure out a plan, see if we could solve the trouble with the throwaways," she said. She was blushing more than before.

"Umm hmm!" Sol said and winked.

With that, the two went silent. *Oh no, do they think I like Dart? I think I like him too. If Sol finds out, he won't stop talking about it,* Suzy thought.

A few hours later, the Silver Sock was starting to close up so they could clean. They were on their way out the door when suddenly, Harf came panting and huffing.

"Quick!... Follow me…" he whispered, breathing heavily and stopping at each word. Sol and Suzy followed him outside. Harf was visibly shaken!

"What's wrong? Catch your breath. Is it bad news?" Sol asked with concern.

"Come with me to the town hall… And hurry!" Harf replied and, with that, dashed in the direction of the hall. Suzy and Sol wanted to ask questions but they knew he wouldn't stop and reply to any. They darted behind the Harf, who stopped only when he reached the town hall and went into the engineering room.

"Quick, get in," he said, gasping, and waited for the two to enter the room. When they did, Harf quickly locked the door behind them.

"I figured out the papers that you've given me, Sol. And it's not good."

Sol and Suzy now looked concerned. Sol was scared

"What did you find?" he asked in a slow voice, shaking.

Harf took a deep breath. "It's a design for a weapon. But not just any weapon," Harf paused. He looked them both in the eyes, which were as terrified as his.

"What?" Sol exclaimed.

"And?" Suzy asked with eyes wide.

Harf grabbed Sol with both hands and exclaimed, "It's a weapon to destroy a sock – forever!!!"

CHAPTER 11
THE STAKES ARE RAISED

Suzy and Sol gasped!

"Are you serious?" asked Sol, almost out of breath. His gaze would jump from Harf to the papers back to Harf. "You can't be serious?"

Harf nodded his head. "I'm very serious," he replied without waiting for both of them to register it completely. He hastily scattered the papers on the table. "Let me show you."

Walking to the table, he pointed to the left corner. "This is a 4-letter cipher. Now, using the recommended components…" he raised his head from the table and saw that both of the socks had a blank expression on their face. They didn't understand one word that Harf was saying. His voice trailed off. "You don't follow me, huh?" he asked.

"I am pretty sure you lost us at the cipher," Suzy replied.

"Oh, right. I see – Well, let me simplify," Harf replied. "A cipher is a disguised way of writing a code."

"Okayyyy…" Suzy said.

Harf didn't quite pay attention to it and continued. "Once I figured out the cipher, it was just a matter of putting the pages in the correct order. Once I did that, it all started to fall into place."

"Yes, exactly something similar. Only, solving this code led me to something very deadly. I was able to rearrange the pages. After rearranging, I was able to piece the various shapes together. It's a machine that apparently can pull a sock apart until there is just a thread left. Do you understand that? JUST A THREAD! And that, too, is me being hopeful. The design here is dangerous, one that even someone crazy like me won't put together! Oh dear! What trouble is looming out there? You'll have to find out quick!"

"Oh no!" exclaimed Suzy, holding her hand to her mouth. "We have to take action right away!"

Harf nodded. He grabbed a chair and sat on the table, focusing his gaze on the scattered pages.

Sol analyzed the situation for a while and decided to take the information he had just received to High Elder. Before he decided to finally dash out, he turned around and faced Harf. "Not a word about this to anyone, Harf. Please!"

"Don't worry, Sol, I won't say anything," said Harf with a low, almost squeaky voice.

With that, Sol and Suzy left the room.

"We have to tell the others," Sol said to Suzy.

"Exactly what I have been thinking," replied Sol, "You get High Elder and Koki. I'll get Sal and Dart. We will meet back at the tower in two hours."

With that, the two split up. Suzy ran to the tower. One of the guards stepped aside and let her in. She was running as fast as she could. Running up the steps, she tapped on High Elder's door. The door opened

"Suzy, why are you here so late and all out of breath? You look like you are here with terrible news of some kind. Is everything okay? Please tell me it is!" Suzy steps in and closes the door.

"One of the engineers…Huff! Huff! Harf! He DECODED the papers Dart found. And I am afraid… Huff! Huff! It is!"

"It is what Suzy! Catch your breath first!"

"It's plans for a weapon. A most terrible weapon." Suzy informed her.

The High Elder looked astonished. "No... this cannot be," she murmured. "What kind of weapon?"

"The most terrible, I am afraid. One that can wipe a sock out of existence! A weapon that can totally unravel a sock!" answered Suzy, her eyes all afraid and wide open.

"We must tell Davet," replied High Elder. "But he is still in Argylonia."

"I was going to get Koki too. We need a plan of action, and we need it now," Suzy replied, concerned.

"Yes, do that," High Elder replied. "I'll meet you all in the safe house."

Suzy nodded and wasted no time and dashed out of the room. The High Elder called in some guards and ordered them to escort her to the safe house. Quickly, a group of lean, tall socks ran after Suzy, who was walking at top speed.

"Huh?" she asked one of them.

"High Elder says you need all the protection you can. Seems like you have some information that needs to be protected!"

Suzy said nothing; only gave a thumbs up. Quickly, she ran off to get Koki. She arrived at his house twenty minutes later. The light of candles could be seen inside.

"Good, he's up," she said to herself. Suzy knocked on the door. The door opened, and Koki stepped outside.

"Suzy! It's rather late," he said with a smile. "Come on in. What's going on?" Suzy shook her head.

"Actually, Koki, you must hurry with me to the safe house per High Elder's request. It's urgent, more urgent than anything we have dealt with so far. I'll explain things on the way!"

"The safe house?" Koki asked. "Why?"

"There is a good chance the throwaways have built the most terrible weapon a sock can face. We are not talking about staff and shields. Something more lethal, something terrible," Suzy replied.

Koki's eyes grew wide, and his face sank a little. "Let's go then, Suzy! Fill me in on the way."

Shortly after, Koki and Suzy reached the safe house. Suzy filled him in on everything. Once inside the safe house, they see Dart, Sol, and Sal.

"High Elder! Suzy filled me in," said Koki.

The High Elder only nodded. "Let's go into my room." The High Elder's room consisted of a bed and a side table. There was a book on the table. There was also a desk with a mirror and a long table with a map of the area. She sat down at the table. The others took their seats. The High Elder motioned for Suzy to report.

Suzy stood up. "The news is that Jol is building a horrible weapon. It's a weapon that can take a sock apart totally. And when we say 'take a sock apart,' we mean down to the last thread. As of now, we don't know how it works. Harf's working on it, but he says the weapon can most easily be the most destructive weapon in East Sockton!"

"We have to find out how far along he is in building it," added Sol. "What we have discovered is only an initial blueprint. There is a lot of room to make it more terrifying than it already is, as Harf has informed us. And if we know anything about Jol, as we all do, he will make it as dangerous as he can, so we must come up with a plan as soon as we can." Dart suddenly stopped and raised his hand to his head as if trying to remember something.

"Dart?" Sol said, "You okay?"

Dart nodded and then facing Koki, said, "Koki and I did see something getting loaded onto a wagon that night."

Koki nodded as if he was remembering the same thing. "I don't know how we forgot that!"

"So, what do we do now?" asked Sal.

The High Elder then stood up. "First," she began, "we have to bring the two throwaways in for questioning."

"That's a great idea," said Arma, the purple sock.

"I agree," said Amawe. She was also a purple sock, just a shade lighter. Everyone looked around, surprised.

"Where did you two come from?" asked High Elder.

Arma chuckles. "We were here the whole time."

Shaking her head, High Elder continued. "Good, more hands on deck. Anyway, then we send scouts out and monitor Jol's area. We may pick up on something. I'm afraid this is some kind of preparation for a possible attack on East Sockton. It makes sense with the throwaways setting up a camp. We must be ready. Suzy, go with Arma and Amawe and scout Warrenark. Dart, go with Suzy."

Nodding, Suzy and Dart leave.

"Koki, you take some guards with you to get Nage and Gamon. Put them in the locking area."

Koki turns and leaves. "Sal and Sol, take Garta and six to eight soldiers and go to the North mountains. Right around here," she points on the map. "We can monitor any throwaway activity in that camp from the higher vantage points. We must be on alert. I think I'll stay here for now. Someone needs to hold the home base."

"But High Elder, we must not leave you alo…" Sal tries to interrupt her, but she waves a hand and stops him.

"I'll be fine. We are taking the offensive. Jol probably won't even realize we are onto his plan."

Nodding, the others turn and leave. The High elder smiled. She realized she couldn't have a better group around her. These socks were the best. But she desperately needed Davet. He was the perfect sock in these areas. She continued to look at the map.

Sal and Sol went to see Garta. Garta was putting some soldiers through some training motions with a staff. The staff was a preferred weapon of the guards. Sal and Sol couldn't help but admire the fluid motions the socks were going through. Sol especially liked Garta. Garta turned and saw them standing there.

"Alright, keep practicing forward motions. I'll be back shortly," she shouted to the socks.

"AYE!" The socks shout in unison.

Garta then joined Sal and Sol. "What's going on, you two?" she asked.

Dart found some papers that some throwaways had. "They are plans to totally unravel a sock – to a single thread!" Sal answered.

"Whoa! Whoa! What?! Easy man, what are you talking about?" Garta replied.

"Exactly!" Sal replied. "The team is already at work, and we need you and some of your men on it too!"

"What actions are being taken?" she said after taking in all the information.

"We are to go with you and eight guards to a vantage point in the North Mountains," Suzy replied. "We have to monitor the throwaway camp from above by order of High Elder."

Garta nodded. "Give me a few minutes," she said. She was always ready for action. She didn't need any more explanation. She quickly ran off and was back in a blink with her battle gear. "I have eight guards ready," she said and motioned a fist to a group of socks standing at a distance in perfect line. They were lean and muscular and marched in excellent formation. All of them had backpacks and staff at the ready.

Garta then started addressing the group. "It's about time we use the training! There is a possible threat lurking in and around the town, and we need to be the eyes and ears. We are to go to the North Mountains and keep watch! There is a throwaway camp being set up outside of town. We are to go and observe. Nothing more. But we will have to be quiet. Understood?"

"Yes, Garta!" they shouted in unison.

Sal and Sol couldn't help but be impressed with Garta's leadership. With that, Garta whistled hard, and three dust horses came galloping at top speeds. She started running along one of them, and with a swift leap, she hopped onto one without stopping the horse and climbing on it.

"Impressive!" Sal said and looked at Sol, who was staring at Garta riding the horse in the distance.

"Keep up!" she yelled without looking back; all socks mounted their dust horses and rode off.

Dart and Suzy met up with Arma and Amawe.

"Hey, Dart," said Arma, smiling. "It's good to see you."

"I agree," said Amawe, also smiling. "Some impressive work you did out there! We have been hearing things," she added with a smile.

Dart turned red. "Thank you very much for your kind words. I had a good teammate in Koki. He was a great help in teaching me."

"Listen," said Suzy, slightly annoyed at the attention they were giving Dart. "We have to go scout Warrenark. And we have to be at our best." She glared at Amawe and Arma.

Arma and Amawe gasped. "We've never scouted Warrenark before!" Arma replied.

"Well, there's a first time for everything," Suzy answered. "We have reason to believe throwaways may be plotting to have a war with us. We have to find out what they are up to besides the weapon. We have to gather as much information as we can."

"Agreed," said Arma. "We have to get some gear. Warrenark will be a challenge."

"We have to even figure out a way to get in," Suzy said, looking confused with a map. "I don't see a way in without getting noticed," she added.

Amawe looked at Arma and smiled. "Well, that is where we come in, friend; we will be right back." The two depart.

Dart watches them walk away. He was still blushing a little. He turns around and sees Suzy glaring at them. "What's wrong, Suzy? The two are quite a pair. And pretty skillful too, from what I heard, aren't they?" he asked.

"Oh... nothing... just thinking," Suzy replied as he saw Dart with a suspicious look. "And yes, the best at what they do. There isn't any place these two cannot sneak in," she added. "Do take notes. They are very thorough."

"I sure will," Dart replied, "Can't miss a thing right now!"

Koki went to the guard barracks. Inside, there were several guards performing gymnastics. One was looped around the loop hanging from the roof. Another was wrapped around the wire of the light that hung from the roof. A staff came flying from behind a long stack of boxes out of nowhere. A slim sock jumped from where the staff came and landed right before the staff hit the ground and caught it.

"Alright boys, gear up. We have to bring in some socks for questioning. Two, to be exact. They are throwaways, but not ordinary ones. They are as dangero..." Koki was giving directions to the group.

"Like you are Koki?" asked one of the guards and was about to snicker when Koki shouted. "NO!" "THEY ARE NOTHING LIKE ME!"

The group of socks was suddenly silent. Koki was hurt, and the group could see it.

"These socks are a threat to this very town, and they are as dangerous as they come! I never have been. And if any of you talk down to me again, you will be expelled from this unit. Understand?"

"Yes, Koki," they replied.

"I'm sorry I said that," the sock replied.

Koki just whirled around and walked out. "Just be outside in 5 minutes," he replied over his shoulder.

Once outside, Koki wiped a tear. It was a tear mixed with rage and sadness. "What do I have to do to get socks to not judge me?" he asked aloud. He figured he would always be judged. Even if he personally threw Jol into a cell in front of the whole town, they wouldn't care. Sighing heavily, Koki just began to focus on the task ahead. Just then, the others joined him outside.

Without another word, all the socks mounted lint horses and rode off.

Sal, Sol, and Garta had reached the vantage point. The place was lonely as if no one had been there in years. There were a lot of wild bushes and trees which had grown way too large and dense. Even though it was daytime, there wasn't much light behind the tree.

It was the perfect cover for observation. Garta immediately had the guards set up camp and took a round piece of glass and a tube out of her backpack. Sal saw that the glass was taken from a pair of glasses. She placed the glass in the tube and placed the instrument on her eye.

"Yup, seems like a camp! They seem active, too!" She said as she saw into the distance with her instrument. "Okay, listen up, here is the plan."

She instructed everyone to be alert at all times. She also assigned rotation and night watch duties to the eight socks. The group waited and watched. She handed Sal and Sol the instrument to see and analyze the place. They did. The other eight socks had their own. Soon, the sun went down, and it was dark.

Sal and Sol were arguing about something.

"You forgot it again. How can you?" Sal was saying

"Why must it always be me?" Sol was trying to defend himself.

"Relax boys. No need to grab each other's throats. We don't want to raise attention toward ourselves. We brought you two some gear too. Here," she grinned and tossed some bedrolls to Sal and Sol.

Sal and Sol grinned back sheepishly. They were glad for Garta because they were in such a rush they didn't even think about supplies. They opened up their bedrolls and slipped in.

Dart, Suzy, Arma, and Amawe had reached the outer edges of Warrenark. A tall fortress with towers along high walls. It looked forbidding in the moonlight. There were a few socks marching on the top with staffs in their hands. Two would occasionally stop and have a chat.

"What now?" Dart asked from behind a bush.

Arma and Amawe just smiled. Arma pointed to an area of the wall that was narrow and looked like a slit from the distance. "Suzy, Amawe, and I will go over the wall there. You will wait here."

"What? Are you crazy? How can you pass through that wall? You'll get caught. Plus, the guards, too, will catch you before you can reach the wall!"

Arma and Amawe snickered and fist-bumped each other.

"Relax," Suzy said, "We have a plan. We'll be okay. We have done this before!"

Suzy came close to Dart, landed both her hands on his shoulders, and said, "If we aren't back by sunrise, go tell High Elder."

"But what if..."

They were gone before the Dart could stop them again!

CHAPTER 12
OTHER PLANS

High Elder and the whole of East Sockton believed that Jol wanted to invade East Sockton simply because he was hateful. His plans were different. Even though some part of the reason was just that, there he had other greater ideas. There was an infamous legend in the sock world about a drifter sock named Galf that was shrouded in mystery and curiosity. It was said that Galf had been trying for years to find a way to link the human world. After many years of trying, he finally found the portal that could help the socks travel between the two worlds. Using the portal, the socks might come through on their own without being lost or thrown away.

Jol was interested in the portal because he wanted to expand his army and followers. His plan was to make sure that whoever comes through that channel in the sock world for the first time, a throwaway can make friends with them and lead them into his following. The idea was that when a sock enters into the sock world, they are lost, helpless, and have no idea of the place and its methods.

He could increase his army. He could then take the fight to Socktopolis, which was two months away, on a lint horse. This was the greatest plan anyone could come up with, and he believed that if he had an army strong enough, he would be one true, undisputed ruler of the sock world.

He received this information from Jargo, a barkeep, who claimed that he had received the information from an elderly sock who claimed he knew where the secret writings were hidden. Plus, the sock said that East Sockton and the surrounding area were popular spots for socks to appear out of nowhere without any information about their whereabouts. This also made Jol believe more in the myth of Galf and the portal that connected the human and the sock world. The elderly sock had said that Galf's work was buried under a rock formation on the cliffs of Axall. Jargo even shared a map that he claimed he received from the elderly rock. That is why Jol increased his efforts and set up a camp so that his army could get to work and he could find the portal before anyone else did.

He left his room and walked down the corridor to his war room. He had a smile on his face as he saw from the windows socks running here and there making arrangements outside. There were socks carrying huge loads and setting up camp. Then, there was a group of socks that was readying all the staff and sticks. Also, there was a group that was setting up something that looked like a foundation of something big. His smile widened at the thought of what would be set up there on the foundation.

When he reached the war room, he saw Chemi lost, looking at some maps scattered on the table. Her hair was all crumpled and twisted. When she looked up and saw Jol coming, she smiled.

"Jol, I have good news. Our camp is almost set up. They should be done in another week." Jol had a small smile on his lips when he entered. He usually didn't smile in front of the socks to appear strict, stern, and angry. When he heard what Chemi said, his smile widened, which shocked Chemi as she didn't remember ever seeing him smile. *Jol rarely smiles,* she thought.

"Excellent! It is about time we increased our efforts, Chemi. Send four of our most trusted soldiers to the cliffs of Axall. Give them this map. Tell them to retrieve anything under the rock formation that's circled."

"Is that where Galf's writings are?" Chemi asked. Jol only smiled back, which gave Chemi the idea that she was correct.

Chemi looked at the map. "Do you think that this is even true, Jol? Galf is a myth. It is not even proven if he even existed."

"Well," said Jol. "It's a chance I'm willing to take. Think of the bigger picture, Chemi. If this is all wrong and false, we lose nothing, but if we are right, we get to rule the whole sock world. Now go get this done."

"Yes, Jol," Chemi replied. "Right away."

Taking the map, she left the room. Jol looked around. *I have to go see someone myself,* he thought. Whirling, he also left the room.

Chemi went to the guard barracks on the other side of Warrenark. There, she saw a heavyset white, gray, and yellow sock named Mafu sitting by some trees. He was a loyal sock and the leader of the elite circle, the small group of highly trained guards that served as Jol's personal protection. They were extremely dangerous and very well-trained. *Mafu was a toad for Jol,* she thought. He was always quick to point out others' mistakes to make himself look good. He would gladly give up anything if Jol wanted him to. She also believed he was trying to take her place. She didn't trust him at all, but she had to put aside her personal feelings. Right now, she was supposed to be focused on the mission.

"Hey, Chemi!" Mafu called out. "What brings you here?"

"Business," she answered. She opened the map. "You are to take three socks with you to the cliffs of Axall to this rock formation," she pointed.

"That is one of the remotest parts of the whole sock world. What do you want us to do there?" Mafu asked in his hoarse, commanding voice.

"Jol, not me. He wants you to look for something. Buried underneath or somewhere close by are a bunch of papers and other things, something that will look like writings and scribblings. Jol needs them."

"Really!" Mafu exclaimed. He was eager to please Jol. "What are the papers about?"

"I don't know," said Chemi, brushing aside the question. "I only do what Jol wants, and right now, he wants these papers and writings. MORE THAN ANYTHING!"

She figured the less everyone knew, the better and safer it was.

"Whatever Jol wants!" Mafu remarked.

Chemi hands him the map. "Jol needs them as soon as possible," she said. "Get it done."

With that, she turned and left. Mafu watched her go. *One day she will get hers!* he thought. *And then Jol will name me second in command.* Mafu left and called out his group of elite guards. He picked out three socks, each built like he was. Heavy set, tall, and ready for action. They assembled gear and left for the cliffs that were several days away.

Chemi was walking across Warrenark back to the main building. She felt like she was being watched. Every now and then, she would stop and look at the tree line to see if someone was hiding there looking at her. From up in a tree, Arma giggled with hands on her mouth, dangling on a branch. She watched Chemi walk away. She and Amawe had heard the whole conversation between Mafu and Chemi, and Amawe had decided that she would follow Mafu while Arma would be on Chemi's tail. Arma kept following Chemi and noted everything she saw. She counted the walls around the main buildings, the entry and exit points, and the number of guards that were posted around the main building. *This must be some important building. The are many guards here – More than what seems necessary. Maybe Jol is in there too!* She thought to herself. When Chemi was around finally at the door of the main building, Arma sneakily wriggled down the tree stump and hid in a thick bush. Figuring she had enough info, she decided she should return back to Suzy.

Amawe was still following Mafu. It was no easy task. Mafu wasn't like Chemi. He was always highly alert. It took all Amawe's skill not to be noticed. She wasn't a fighter. If Mafu discovered her, she would have no chance against him. She took every step with extra caution. But it didn't scare her as she had done similar jobs many times before. Mafu went to a smaller building. It was where the elite circle stayed. The group had a separate place from the regular guards. Amawe tiptoed behind the bushes lined along the route and went for Mafu to go inside. Seeing a window partially open, she crept up to hear what was going on inside. At first, she heard sticks being cracked and soldiers training,

"Hiyaa! Ten sticks, brother. That is a new record!" A heavy voice called!

"Ten sticks with one blow! Man, you are getting stronger and fiercer every day!" Another similar voice replied. "Now, watch me. I will climb this wall in just 5 seconds and land on this table."

It was an all-grey sock. He tapped on the table that was as thin as one of the staff the guard usually carried. There were papers, sticks, and lanterns scattered on the table. With that, the grey sock ran and jumped on the building. There were small rocks protruding out of the wall, which he used as stepping stones, and he climbed to the top before Amawe could count. When at the top, he jumped and landed on the table without the table even making a creaking sound.

"Woah! That is what I am talking about!" The first one came and high-fived this grey sock.

Amawe was amazed at the skill.

Seeing Mafu arrive, the socks assembled themselves. Out of the shadows, two more socks came and joined the first two as one of them said, "Huddle up! Mafu's here. Time to get to work."

Mafu joined the group and started speaking in a low voice. The conversation was muffled. Amawe was able to make out bits and pieces. Something about "We will leave in the morning," she heard Mafu say. Thinking she had enough info, Amawe turned and left for the rendezvous point. Suzy was having no luck at all. She had chosen to stay behind to follow Jol. She saw him enter a canteen. She knew she couldn't go inside. Some time passed. Jol didn't come out. Disappointed, she turned to leave. *Maybe the others had more luck,* she figured.

Koki and his soldiers arrived at Nage and Gamon's house. They dismounted their lint horses, and the two went to the back door while Koki and the sock, who had spoken with him earlier, went to the front.

"I really am sorry, Koki," he said again.

"No worries, that's nothing new for me. Let's just concentrate on this mission," he replied.

On the count of five, they kicked in the door and charged inside. Nage and Gamon looked surprised.

"What's going on?" asked Nage. At first, he was taken by surprise and wanted to dash out of the doorway after pushing the two socks standing near it. Then he saw Koki and stopped right away. He smirked and said, "Wait! Is that you, Koki? Look, Gamon, it's the mighty Koki," he laughed.

"Jol will be glad to see you. What brings you here? Who are your friends?" asked Gamon. Koki sees the other guards come into the room.

"Nage and Gamon!" he exclaimed. "You are under arrest for plotting against East Sockton. You are to come with us!"

"Plotting?" said Nage. "What do you mean?"

"Not another word," Koki replied. Nodding to the guards, Koki motioned for them to tie Nage and Gamon's hands up. Gamon laughed.

"You are really arresting your fellow throwaways?" he asked. "Surely you can't be serious," he added with a rude expression followed by a wide smile.

"I am very serious," Koki replied, a little annoyed.

"Don't worry, Gamon," said Nage. "Koki will come to his senses. Eventually, he will figure out these socks are using him. He will let us go. Won't you? BROTHER!"

"Shut up! I am in my right senses. If there is anyone who is not, it is you. Raging war on peace-loving socks." Koki retorted, then gently pushed him and said, "And I am not your brother."

The other socks then escorted Nage and Gamon out of the room. Koki just stood there shaking his head. He couldn't afford seeds to be planted.

Sal and Sol were sitting at a table playing cards. They heard rustling through the brush. Looking up, they see Garta coming through. "Nothing is going on at the moment. I guess we just wait," she said.

"I wonder how the others are doing?" Sal asked.

"Having better luck for sure," remarked Sol. "Anyway, we have constant surveillance on them down there." Garta motioned. "I don't like waiting."

"No one does," Sal replied. "But orders are orders."

Back at the safe house, High Elder was in her room looking at a map. She was trying to join the bits and pieces together and was focused on the scatter in front of her when she heard rumpus from outside. She looked out the window and saw Koki and a team of her elite guards bringing two socks in ropes. She quickly ran to join Koki.

"You two must be Nage and Gamon," she said. "We have a lot of questions for you."

Gamon smirked. "But I am afraid we don't have any answers for you. Plus, make sure you ask your questions while we are here because we won't be here long. We have Koki. He will come to his senses. He will let us out."

"That'll never happen," Koki said, smiling, "You two are on the wrong side. You'll see."

"Are we Koki?" Nage shot back. "Look around you. You think this all matters, and this will change the way they look at you. This is all for nothing. These socks don't care about you." He

"ENOUGH!" said Koki. "Lock those two up. Do not listen to the lies they are spewing." The guards escorted Nage and Gamon away.

"We will be waiting, Koki! Don't disappoint us!" Nage shouted as he was being taken away.

"Once a THROWAWAY, always a THROWAWAY friend, don't forget that!" Gamon joined Nage. Both laughed in unison.

"Don't worry, Koki," High Elder came and rested her hand on Koki's shoulder, "They are just desperate, is all. They are trying to get you angry and make you do something stupid! You are one of us! Always have been, always will be."

"Thank you, High Elder!" He said, but didn't sound very sure. He just shook his head, waited for High Elder to drop her hand, and then left the room. As Koki walked, he could still hear the wild laughter of Nage and Gamon coming from the building.

CHAPTER 13
DIRE DOINGS

Dart paced behind the bushes nervously, peeking every now and then to see if either of the two had returned. His heart was racing, and he was on high alert. He finally sat down behind a bush.

"I think it is too late now. I think they got caught! What do I do now? Think, Dart! Think!" Dart whispered to himself. "Maybe I should go tell High Elder. Or maybe I should wait a little more? Maybe I should go after them! Yes, that sounds like a plan!"

He picked a stick and started drawing on the ground.

"Ok, so this is where the guards are…." He scribbled a building with a tower and made a mark, then continued, "And this is the door… Here, we have another guard, and both these guards move in about twenty seconds. This will give meee… Umm.. At least… Ten seconds to go unnoti…"

"We can do it in eight!" two voices spoke at the same time which jolted Dart and made him jump.

"Woah! When did… How did you guys? You guys scared me!" Dart said, collecting himself. It was Amawe and Arma puffing and smiling, standing next to her. "I didn't even hear or see you guys coming! What took you so long? I was afraid you two got cau…"

"Caught? Nope. Not us," Arma said and fist-bumped Amawe, who returned a wink.

Dart was relieved to see the two back and in good health. "So, what did you find out?" he asked.

"Apparently, Jol sent some soldiers to the Cliffs of Axall for something we are aware of. They are on to something. Something big, I am sure. That is not a part you want to visit!" Arma replied with worry.

"And that is only half of the news. The other terrifying bit is that one of the soldiers is an old warrior named Mafu," Amawe added. She looked worried. "He is fearsome and strong. He is one of the strongest warriors in the world of socks. He has made himself quite a name for fighting many socks at once."

Dart listened attentively. "Well, it doesn't matter much, does it? Jol doesn't realize we know some of his plans. As long as we do a good job of hiding, we will be able to figure out what he's up to."

Just then, Suzy appeared, and seeing the three on high alert and worried, she asked, "What did you find out? It looks like you three have some bad news."

"Well, we found out he is sending some soldiers to the Cliffs of Axall for some reason," Arma replied and then added, "Did you find something useful?"

Suzy just shook her head. "Nothing at all. Jol went into a small building and didn't come out. I waited but realized he wasn't coming out anytime soon, so I left."

"Okay, now this all doesn't make sense. Something is definitely up, and we need to act now," said Dart. The three nodded in agreement. He then suggested, "Let's just go back to the safe house. We can regroup there and share it with the rest of the team. I am sure they'll have some ideas and insights to share on what we have found."

Without any further discussion, they quickly rounded up their stuff and set off for the lengthy journey back.

Two bulky guards with staffs and in full body armor were standing by the cell that held Nage and Gamon. Koki walked in with High Elder. Both the guards tapped their staffs on the floor twice, bowed, and moved to the sides. Nage looked up.

"Koki, old friend! You've come to let us out, aren't you, buddy?" he grinned. "See, Gamon, I told you Koki would come to his senses."

Koki ignored him.

"Who else is in this plot with you," he simply asked.

"Plot?... What plot?" replied Gamon.

Koki unrolled the sheets he held in his hand and shoved them in front of the two from across the door. It was the same papers Dart found.

"These were found in your home," he replied. "They are plans for some kind of machine that can destroy a sock forever. "

Nage and Gamon went pale as they inspected the drawings.

"Yeah, that's what I thought. We know more than you think we do!" Koki declared and smiled, looking at the two of them get concerned.

"If you are smart, which I think you both would love to call yourself, you two will cooperate one way or another," The High Elder added in.

Koki grinned at them. "Think about it; you can still have a way out if you want!"

As Koki turned and was about to leave, he instructed the guards, "You both stay alert!" The two guards nodded and then thumped their staffs and went back to their positions.

Just when Koki was about to leave, Gamon's voice echoed in the cell, "It's ok, Koki! Eventually, Jol will get us, and you know it too. If you have any of the brains we heard you have, you would go talk to him immediately. He will accept you back, trust me!"

"Oh, that is very generous, but I think I will stay here, guys. I have a greater purpose. And that is to protect everyone in this town from Jol." With that, Koki turned and left the room. Outside, he sees High Elder.

"I have to get some sleep," he said. "I should go home."

The High Elder nodded. "Yes, you've been working more than you should. I'll go to my tower. Great job, Koki!" With that, they both left the room.

"What do we do now?" Gamon asked Nage.

"Now, we wait!" Nage replied. His eyes, which were previously fixed at Koki, were now fixed at the door Koki had left through.

The next day, Koki went to the tower. He had to meet with High Elder.

"Koki, good morning. Slept well?" she smiled and asked.

"Good morning. Only for a few hours, I couldn't sleep. I was up thinking what to do with the two and what we should do next. There isn't much we know about Jol's plan." Koki replied with concern in his voice.

High Elder waved him toward a chair.

"Did you think of our next step?" he asked as he went towards the chair.

She nodded. "Well, the festival is starting today, which means, for three days, the town is celebrating. I think we take advantage of keeping up appearances, to maybe listen to the talk and such. I am sure Jol will see this as an opportunity too, and will send his socks over here to make his move. Plus, we can start setting up perimeters around the outskirts without too much suspicion. We don't need to start a panic."

Koki nodded in agreement. "That's a good idea. Those two locked up can sit for a while. It might get them to talk."

"Sounds like a plan," High Elder said and then asked, "Any word from the rest of the team?"

"Suzy and the others should return soon enough. I am sure they will have something we can work on, and no more about what Jol is up to," Koki replied.

"Excellent. I will give the orders." High Elder informed.

"I will go make sure the security is on high alert and ready for any action," Koki replied and went out.

Koki spent the day making his rounds. He dispatched a unit to monitor the outskirts of town disguised as commoner sock folks. He had them set up stations with equipment and horses. They had to be ready just in case Jol made a move. Meanwhile, High Elder, too, was drafting up plans for defenses. She sent out some socks to travel to Argylonia to find Davet. He would be a key in this. She was tired and started thinking of giving Davet the reins of the town. Now, with all this happening, she put the plans on hold.

Later that day, Suzy and the others arrived back at the safe house. Seeing no one there, they went to the tower. The High Elder was glad to see them.

"Oh, finally, you guys are back. We have been waiting. Do you have any news?" she asked without waiting for any greetings.

Dart nodded. "Not a good one, apparently. Jol has sent some of his elite circle, under the leadership of some sock named Mafu, to the Cliffs of Axall to retrieve something. I have been told he is a legendary warrior. We don't know what that something is. Arma and Amawe did a fine job of finding this information. Suzy also discovered that Jol was working on something in his small building. Maybe it is the machine we found the pictures of in Nage's house."

The High Elder plopped down in her chair and thought for a moment. The other three waited for her to give further instructions.

"Cliffs of Axall? Now, why would anyone even think about going there? At least no sane sock would do that. But I guess someone like Jol would surely have something going on in such a remote part. We must expect anything from him," she spoke softly to herself.

"Tomorrow, can you all go to Axall? Scout out the town, maybe? Jol is setting up a base there. He would have access to the water," High Elder spoke after a long pause. "Except you Dart. I need you here."

Suzy and the others nodded.

"Alright then," said High Elder. "It's settled. But first, I want you to go attend the festival and see if we have any of Jol's guys already in town. I suspect they are. Arma and Amawe, I am counting on you two for this one. Suzy, be watchful and see if you notice someone out of the ordinary or acting strange."

Suzy, Arma, and Amawe nodded, said Goodbye, and left. Dart remained behind.

"Dart, I will need you to go to the encampment at the end of the week and meet up with Sal and Sol. I don't have a good feeling about it, and we need to be prepared for the worst. Stay for a few days with them and collect as much information as you possibly can. I am counting on your judgment to try to figure out how all the activities are connected. Bring these maps and start setting up more stakeout spots if you have to, but make sure these stakeouts are hidden from plain sight. We cannot risk being seen. We can set up an attack from them if necessary, but we need to be prepared for it and know where exactly we need to mount our defenses. Let me know if we have to move on the throwaways."

Dart took the maps from High Elder.

"In the meantime, work with Koki to set up the defenses around town." She added more instructions

"On it, High Elder. I will do my best," Dart agreed.

"I am sure you will." High Elder encouraged him.

Dart turned and left the room. Going outside, Dart realized how far he had come after joining High Elder's inner circle. If he hadn't, he would have been just like the other town socks, who didn't have an idea of the looming threat. He thought to himself, *Wow, this spy work really is some hush-hush work. If I wasn't part of the team, I would have thought, why wouldn't they tell everyone about such a weapon being made by the enemy? But now, it makes complete sense not to share this information with the socks. They will surely panic, and we cannot afford that right now. I guess that is the best way to deal with a dangerous situation. To not panic when trouble is around.*

Dart went to the festival. It was a big event. There were stands set up for socks to play games. The whole town was out there making merry. There were socks running around, laughing and enjoying the rides. There were tree-swing rides, story circles, and lively music all over. There was a sock that Dart found very fascinating who was juggling eight balls while riding a unicycle. Then there was another that had almost ten hula hoops around his waists, and he was dancing to the music, swinging the hoops. Socks were sitting at tables and on grass. Everyone was having a really good time.

Walking around, Dart saw Suzy with Koki. They smiled as he approached.

"Hey all, how are you?" Suzy giggled. "Koki just lost to a can toppling game to yours truly."

Koki rolled his eyes. "I didn't. She clearly cheated."

They all laughed.

"This might be all the fun I'll have right now," said Suzy.

"That's a long ride to Axall. But I'll leave tonight." Koki nodded in agreement. "Suzy filled me in. I'll assign 5 of my guards to go with you. If necessary, they should be able to handle anything Mafu has. But for now, I want a rematch with you."

Suzy laughed. "Sure, I don't mind beating you once more." They all walk back to the games.

CHAPTER 14
TROUBLE IN THE RANKS

Mafu and his soldiers reach the cliffs six days later. It was a long and tiring hike. The moment they reached the cliff, the soldiers dropped all their belongings and crashed on the gravel and the rocks. They took in the sweet-smelling sea breeze for a little while.

"Oof! That was… huff…huff…exhausting!" one of the soldiers said.

"Sure it… huff…was…Why are we here…huff…huff…anyway?"

"Because Jol ordered us to, and that is all the reason we need. Listen here! Don't be lazy, or we will get in trouble! We do what we are told. We find those papers or scribblings, whatever they are, and we take them back. And we better hurry! This isn't a vacation! And we have to cover a lot of ground!" Mafu ordered in his gruffest voice.

For Mafu, it was a breezy and sunny day outside as he looked down at the Parsal Sea. He hadn't picked up much luggage and was quite refreshed compared to the rest of his teammates. Back at Warrenark, he often thought of giving up his current life and going sailing. He fondly remembered sitting at an old drinking shack and listening to the sailors talk about life in the salty air. *Oh, what fun would that be! Me, with the dolphin cawing behind – the seagulls too! Soon, one day!* He thought to himself as he gazed at the sea in the distance as dolphins jumped out of the water and went back in playfully. He smiled for a moment then, but soon, that smile turned into a mean grin.

"But only after I am made his second in command. I deserve it. Maybe even more power later, but for now, being the second in command works for me." He whispered to himself.

Jol's promise of making him the second in command has kept Mafu from leaving Warrenark. Suddenly, he heard a voice calling his name.

"Captain! Captain Mafu! Here!" one of the soldiers was frantically waving his hand.

"Huh?" he said, turning around.

"What does this formation look like? Can you give us a little idea? It is difficult to find something unless we know what we are looking for!" the guard shouted with a huffed, tired voice.

Mafu pulled out the map. "Oh well, yes, I almost forgot!" he unfolded the map, which was almost crumpled, and pointed at one messed-up image. "It looks like this! This jagged formation. Can you see it?" he said, pointing at one.

"How can we see it from this far? Plus, the map is all crumpled. I cannot make out a single thing on it!" one sock grumbled. Knowing that there wasn't much to be known from the map, the socks still carefully looked at it, memorized whatever they could, and went back looking.

They were helpless and didn't have a single idea of what to look for. They foolishly looked around. There were rock formations in every direction they saw. They all had different shapes, and they blended together. Every formation first looked like the one on the map. Even Mafu knew it would be difficult to find what they were looking for in such a scattered place. They searched for two hours without taking a break. Whenever they thought they had found the one formation they were looking for, someone would point out a difference, and they would have to look all over again.

Mafu was getting frustrated. "This couldn't possibly be this hard!" he shouted. The socks instantly became more vigilant and started looking at each rock formation more carefully. An hour went by and not a sign of the rock formation was in sight. Mafu's soldiers were getting anxious. They knew better than to make Mafu angry. Suddenly, a sock named Murn came across a formation that looked like the one on the map. He inspected it carefully, going around it three to four times. Once he was sure that it was the rock formation he was looking for, he shouted with a wide smile on his face.

"Here it is!" Jumping and waving his hand to the other socks, he yelled as loud as he could.

Mafu and the others ran over to where Murn was standing. Mafu quickly pulled out the map, stretched it out, and started looking at the formation. He cross-checked all the details, and when he was sure it was the one, he took a sigh of relief and patted Murn heavily on the back.

"Well done! I knew you would find it. Okay, all of you now! Start digging," he said without missing a beat.

The other socks quickly ran over to their backpacks, pulled out their spades, and got to work. Even though they were tired, finally finding the rock formation had excited them.

Back in town, Suzy and the others had begun their ride to Axall. Suzy wanted to go after them right after Amawe had brought the information, but High Elder had ordered them to wait. Suzy knew that waiting would give Mafu a head-start of a few several days, but High Elder was an experienced leader, and Suzy knew that if she had asked to wait, it surely would be the right thing to do. Suzy knew they couldn't possibly catch up. Besides, High Elder just wanted them to observe and act if necessary.

The digging went on for several hours, but nothing came up. Now, even Mafu was exhausted. They were sweating, and the dry air was now making it difficult to breathe. Every now and then, one of them would cough heavily and crash, only to be shouted at by Mafu. After searching in several spots around the formation, Mafu just about gave up. He didn't even know what they were looking for or for what reason. He just knew it was important to Jol, and he didn't want to disappoint his leader. He sat on a rock, thinking what he could do when a cream-colored sock named Murf stabbed his spade into the ground with all his might.

"Thud! Crack." A woody sound came.

"I think I found something!" Murf exclaimed. Immediately, every sock was at their toes. They had their eyes fixed on Murf now. Mafu got up and ran.

"Hit it again!" he ordered, and sure enough, another cracking sound came, this time louder.

As Murf pulled out his spade, a wooden chunk came back with it. A broken wooden box could be seen peeking from under the ground. All the socks got down on their knees instantly and started removing the dirt with their hands.

"Well, hurry and uncover the rest of it," ordered Mafu, who was now excited and alert.

In a few minutes, the socks uncovered the box. Murf pulled it out and passed it to Mafu, who opened it gleefully, surprised and excited. He opened the box and found a dark rock among many others, along with a large pile of papers. As soon as the sunlight hit the rock, the seemingly dark rock started glowing brightly, shining like a star, brighter than anything the socks had ever seen. The socks covered their eyes, and Mafu quickly grabbed the papers out of the box and closed the lid again. The rock glowed for a little while, with light coming out of the broken box, but then it went dark again. Mafu began reading the papers.

"Glig…Endi…liigg," Mafu struggled to make sense of the words but couldn't.

After a few minutes of trying, Mafu suddenly realized what he was looking at. His mouth opened wide. "These are the notes of

Galf!" His eyes were wide open as he looked at the papers, and his hands trembled.

"Galf? Who is Galf?" Murn asked.

"Galf was one legendary wise old sock. Legend has it that he had figured out a way to join our former world with our own," replied Mafu.

"I thought he was a myth!" One of the sock intervened

Mafu looked up and was in complete shock, but he quickly folded the papers. He took a deep breath and settled himself down. *He obviously was real*, he remarked to himself. Suddenly, he had a wicked smile on his face.

"We must get these back to Jol right away…unless…" he declared

"Unless what?" Murn asked.

Mafu had a daring idea. "Unless Jol signs a document banishing Chemi and making me the vice leader," Mafu replied.

Murn and the others couldn't believe what they were hearing. They were confused and surprised. Mafu had never before bargained with Jol and did everything just as he was told.

"Jol isn't going to go along with it, will he? Chemi has been his associate for a long time. She trusts her too much," Murn remarked.

"Oh, he will. He doesn't have a choice now, does he? If he wants these papers and stones, he will do it," Mafu replied, grinning like a fox.

Mafu looks at a green, yellow, and blue colored sock. "Guha! You are to go back to Warrenark and give Jol my demands. Only until I see the signed paper with HIS seal will I give him these."

"But Chemi is irreplaceable to Jol, he won't…" began Guha.

"I AM IRREPLACEABLE!" Mafu roared without letting Guha finish and towered over Guha. "NOT CHEMI!! ME, THE MIGHTY MAFU, I AM IRREPLACABLE, YOU HEAR? I DESERVE TO BE THE VICE LEADER. I PUT IN MY TIME AND AM SUPERIOR TO CHEMI IN EVERY WAY! YOU DO EXACTLY LIKE I SAY! CLEAR?"

"I'm sorry, sir," Guha mumbled while trembling. "You surely are irreplaceable! I will… I will… leave right away, good sir."

"Excellent! And hush now. As fast as you could," said Mafu. "The rest of us will stay behind in Axall and await your return."

Guha dashed and was out of sight before Mafu could roar and yell again.

Guha arrived in Warrenark some days later. On his ride, he thought about how to approach Jol with the news. He dreaded every minute. He figured the best way was to tell him outright. Nodding to some of the guards, he went to Jol's chambers. He knocked on the door.

"Come in," Jol replied without looking up from the table he was working on. Guha went in, walked up to Jol, and saluted.

"Where is Mafu? Why isn't he here himself? Don't tell me he got caught too!" said Jol.

Guha gulped loudly and began, "He... he..." his words were shaky.

"Speak louder and quickly. We don't have the whole day. WHERE IS MAFU?" Jol's voice shook the very place they were standing in.

Gahu flinched at the sudden order and began speaking again, this time as loud as he could, "Mafu stayed behind in Warrenark, sir."

Jol's eyes narrowed. "And why is that? Did you all find what I sent you for?"

Guha nodded.

"Well, where are the papers? Did you lose them? Cause if you did..." Mafu asked.

"No, no, Sir, we didn't lose the papers!" Guha began. "Mafu said you can't have the papers..."

"WHAT? HAS HE LOST HIS MIND?" Jol got up and barged in Gahu's direction, who quickly took a step back and cowered.

"He said that unless you sign a paper banishing Chemi and making him Vice Leader, you can forget the papers!" Gahu completed his sentence with a shaking voice.

Jol only stared in disbelief. "Mafu dares to be insolent? At a time like this?" he said to himself. Guha expected the Jol to react just like he was.

"Mafu also wants me to deliver the papers so you can sign them, and then I am ordered to take them back to him," Gahu added, maintaining his distance.

Jol chuckled. "And what do you think I should do, Guha? Do you think Mafu should be the new Vice Leader?"

"No sir," Guha replied. "I'm fine with things the way they are. I even told Mafu he was making a mistake."

"Good answer," said Jol, and he laid his huge hand on Guha's head, which was now a little relieved. Guha, like many others, was quite happy with Chemi as their Vice Leader. Guha especially respected Chemi because she had helped him a lot and saved him many times from Jol. She helped him become who he was. Looking at Guha, he knew what needed to be done.

"Go to your building, Guha. I need you to take over as the new leader of the Elite Circle." Guha's eyes widened. "Y-y-yes s-s-sir," he stammered. He had no idea how to react. He was scared and surprised at the same time, but he didn't dare say no to Jol, especially an angry Jol. Saluting, he walked out of the room. Jol just shook his head. He never thought Mafu would do something like this, but Chemi did. It was she who suggested to Jol that Mafu must be followed in case there was a problem. Jol felt thankful to Chemi.

He went to a window and opened a cage that had a lint pigeon in it. Jol quickly grabbed a paper and angrily scribbled a note. He tied it to one of the pigeon's legs and then whispered something in its ears. He kept mumbling something in the pigeon's ear for a while and then plunged it into the air. The pigeon began its journey toward Axall.

CHAPTER 15
THE ENFORCER

After almost flying for the day, the pigeon reached a spot not far from the outskirts of Axall, near a lone tent hidden from sight. A green sock, fully cloaked with a hood, came out. It took the message from its leg and read it. It smiled.

"Finally, some action!" Some time ago, the sock was riding past Warrenark. Four socks were outside. They called it some funny name and then laughed. The cloaked figure then quickly took down all four of them. Jol happened to be there and was so impressed he hired the sock on the spot.

"Welcome to my world!" Jol exclaimed and shook its hand. The sock, who made a living enforcing, accepted Jol's handshake.

Now, It had received its first assignment. Taking down a member of Jol's circle. The sock reflected on past conquests: How it traveled around as a loner. Not loyal to anyone. It was just out to collect an occasional bounty. It wasn't above the law, but it didn't exactly follow it.

That night, the sock entered Axall. There was a drink shack that was very popular not too far away. The sock figured Mafu would be there. The sock reached the building and looked in. There were about thirty socks in there.

It walked through the door. The music was loud, and everyone seemed to be having a good time. There was a bunch of sailor socks singing the chorus "To the sea, we belong!" as loud as they could. They looked cheerful. There were also a bunch of sailors telling sea stories.

"We surf the biggest wave you would have ever seen! It almost threw us on the rocks!" one of them said.

Normally, the cloaked sock would've sat and listened to the stories. But this wasn't one of those times. It looked toward the bar, and suddenly, its gaze settled on someone who looked like the drawing of the sock the pigeon had brought. It was Mafu.

"Found you!" it grinned.

No one paid much mind to the cloaked figure slowly walking up to the bar. The sailors there didn't care much for anyone except themselves. Mafu had his back turned to the sock. He was sipping a drink and was rocking side to side in his chair. When the cloaked, green sock reached Mafu, it heard him humming a tone. He tapped Mafu on the shoulder.

"Go away," Mafu said without looking back. He had a wide smile on his face and was looking down at his drink. The sock tapped him again, stronger this time. Mafu twirled around.

"Look! I said I don't want to be bothered."

He stared at the sock and realized it wasn't from around there.

"The papers," the green sock simply said with a strong, hoarse, and husky voice.

"What?" Mafu asked in disbelief.

"The papers," the sock repeated. "Jol wants them."

Mafu stared in disbelief but then broke into a drunken laughter

"So, Jol sent someone like you to take something from me?"

"Is there a problem, Mafu?" asked Murn, who appeared out of nowhere, anchored himself next to the cloaked sock, and folded his arms.

"This sock was sent by Jol to get our papers," Mafu replied, chuckling. He laughed for a while, but suddenly, the smile vanished, and he sternly said, "But what's worse, Jol clearly took Chemi's side."

He turned toward the cloaked sock and remarked, "Well, in that case, you can go and tell Jol he will never see these papers."

"Not good enough. I have been paid already, and I am not returning without them!" the cloaked figure replied. Murn got into action and shoved the cloaked figure back. The cloaked figure took Murn's arm and twisted his wrist, forcing him to bend over. Murn never saw the kick coming. He just crashed to the floor and lay there with his eyes closed. The music stopped, and everyone just stared. Just then, the other guards rushed toward the cloaked figure, grabbed it tightly, and dragged it outside. Everyone inside then heard grunting and crashing. Mafu laughed.

"Should have listened to me!" he said and waited for his guard to return. Instead, the door swung open, and the cloaked figure came back in.

Seeing it, the smile disappeared from his face, and he got up from his seat.

"Just come and get them!" he yelled.

The cloaked figure ran and jumped at Mafu. He ducked and punched him in the stomach.

"How do you like that? You think you can take on the mighty Mafu?" he screamed as he threw another punch at the cloaked sock.

This time, the cloaked sock was quick, dodged Mafu's fist, and then jumped back. It steadied itself and then charged again but stopped short as Mafu swung its leg. Mafu thought that the kick would down it once and for all but was caught by surprise when the cloaked sock moved like lightning and grabbed the leg before it went down. It pulled hard and lunged Mafu forward. Before Mafu could raise his hands, the green sock threw a punch that smashed into Mafu's face. The hit made Mafu groggy, and before he could steady himself, the cloaked sock lifted him up, crashed him on the table once, and then shoved him on the floor. Mafu was out and lying next to Murn. The cloaked figure looked around. No one moved.

"Where are this sock's belongings at?" it said in a low voice.

One sailor just pointed outside and gulped.

"Those socks are staying in that small house two doors down." The owner of the bar said.

The cloaked figure nodded thanks, then left. Soon, it was riding away from town with the box tied to its horse. It rode back to camp. After putting the box in a corner of the tent, it went to sleep. As it rolled over, there was a glint of silver in the moonlight.

The next morning, the cloaked sock was up before the crack of the first ray of sunlight. It quickly readied its stuff, stowed everything firmly on its horse, and took off for Warrenark. The ride was uneventful.

"I should go West if I have to get away from this place. I have heard it is beautiful!" It murmured to itself as he rode through the long route.

The cloaked figure finally arrived back at Warrenark. It rode into the courtyard, got off the horse, and handed the reins to a stable sock. It grabbed the box and walked inside. It was stopped at the door of a chamber where a guard stopped him.

"I have something that belongs to Jol, but I will only give it to him." It told the guard, who sized it up and down and then nodded and opened the door.

"Well," said Jol, seeing the sock. "Were you successful?"

The sock simply held up the box. Jol was delighted.

"Good. Excellent! I never had a doubt!" he exclaimed. "Your payment shall be given. I have some more work for you if you are willing."

The cloaked sock nodded its head.

"Excellent! I knew the first time I looked at you that you were useful. Tomorrow, can you go to my encampment? I'll show you where it is on a map." Jol clapped his hand and continued eagerly without much delay.

The figure nodded.

"That's good," Jol said.

He called a guard over.

"See to it that our guest is taken care of. Anything it asks for, - it must be given. Consider them my needs. No complaints!"

The guard saluted. "Yes sir!" and ushered the cloaked figure towards the door.

Jol watched them depart. As soon as the door closed, he let out a laugh.

"These papers will be the downfall of the lost. Finally, I will have the whole world under my command! This calls for a celebration."

Later that day, Jol went out to a drink house and sat at a corner table, drinking his favorite drink, turnip juice. But he wasn't just out there to celebrate. He was also waiting to meet Chemi. Chemi walked through the door. Jol smiled. *Always on time,* he thought. Sitting down, she immediately told a news that would alarm Jol.

"Nage and Gamon have been captured."

Jol jumped up from his seat. "WHAT DO YOU MEAN?" he roared.

Chemi nodded. "We had a few socks go to see what other information was collected and keep an eye on the town. There, they saw Nage and Gamon being taken away in cuffs by a few guards."

"No!" said Jol, "This can't be."

Chemi gave him a look. "And there's worse news."

"Worse? Worse than this?" Jol asked. "What can possibly be worse?"

"Koki was one of the guards taking them away."

"Koki?" Jol was astonished. "Koki is working with the lost? So, it was true." Jol had heard rumors, but they were never confirmed. He got back into the seat and calmed himself with the drink he had in front of him. "I thought he was long gone. How can this be?" he muttered.

Chemi shook her head. "I told you not to send him away, Jol. He was resourceful and could be used."

Jol just slumped into his seat. He started estimating the risks and how his plans could be wasted if Koki was working with the lost. He realized that this made his conquest even harder. Jol knew Koki was a seasoned warrior, one of the best he had ever worked with. Jol knew that only he himself could ever beat him in a fight; no one else could. He was sure about that. And that, too, if he got lucky. Jol sat in pin-drop silence. He thought hard. There was only the sound of Jol gulping the turnip juice. Then it occurred to him. And that could work for sure.

There was a good way to free Nage and Gamon. It would take some daring, but he had someone who might be able to help. Someone whom he didn't fully trust but let him stay at Warrenark just in case he was useful. The sock already wanted to be a part of what he figured was Jol's inevitable reign. Jol had convinced him about that.

Jol had figured he had nothing to lose with this option.

"Come on, Chemi, let's go talk to our new "friend.""

Chemi stood without much conversation. She knew where they were going. She didn't like the idea but didn't say much. There was a risk, she knew, but they didn't have many options now that Mafu had betrayed them.

Jol and Chemi left the bar and walked to a holding area. It was in the remotest places in Warrenark and heavily guarded. The holding area was a tall building that looked like a fortress and was made of black stone. There were two guards stationed at the door of a cell. Jol nodded to the guards, who saluted and then walked away. Jol pulled out a bunch of keys and unlocked the door.

"Would you be interested in a spot on the team? You might be getting bored here. I have a job, and there is no one better out there, I think, who could do it like you can!"

A familiar red and blue sock stepped out. It was Davet. Davet just smiled

"Whatever you want, Jol."

CHAPTER 16
THE TRAITOR IN THE RANKS

Jol stared at him. "You expressed interest in joining me. You are part of the lost, which is a crime in itself, but if you want to prove yourself, I have a job for you."

"I am listening," Davet, the red and blue sock, replied eagerly.

Jol continued, "Two throwaways were captured by Koki. I am sure you know about him and the relationship we HAD with him. Well, anyway, I wouldn't delve into it much. Here is what is important. Two of my socks, their names are Nage and Gamon. Return them here, and then we'll talk. Understand?"

"I understand, Jol," replied Davet.

Jol nodded his head. "Now go! And don't dare to play me!"

Davet bowed, grinning.

Jol summoned a guard. "Show our "friend" out."

Chemi understood the way Jol used the term friend was sarcastic and thus knew that Jol would surely have something in mind if he was letting out a mischief-monger like Davet, yet knowing Davet, she was a bit concerned, which was evident from the burrow on her forehead.

"Follow me," the guard ordered Davet.

"Let's get to work then," Davet murmured, stretched, and followed the guard out of the room.

As soon as they were gone, Chemi turned to Jol and, with a concerned and serious expression, asked, "You don't intend to bring him on board with us, do you?"

Jol laughed and assured her, "He is willing to betray his own group, his friends. To me, that's the worst kind of sock. What makes you think he would be loyal to us? I want to use him because East Sockton folks might believe him easily, and they are always ready to give their friends a chance. Makes him a good candidate to get Nage and Gamon out. If he delivers – good, we will give him a few more jobs. If he doesn't, well, how difficult is it to get rid of him, right? Maybe he will become the first one we use our weapon on. Along with Koki, that is."

Chemi just laughed, trying her best to hide her nervousness.

Davet left Warrenark with different visions. He was angry about being locked up. Now, he had revenge in his heart. He knew the throwaways were capable of waging war with the lost, something he tried to warn High Elder. But she didn't want to listen. He thought it was a grave mistake. She even allowed them to come to East Sockton, which, according to Davet, was a graver mistake. Davet noticed Koki didn't seem to mind.

Davet felt that, being such a senior member of High Elder's team, she should have listened to him. But she didn't. Davet decided he wasn't going to be on a losing team, so he figured he had to take matters into his own hands. He decided to change sides. *If Koki could do it, then surely I could too; what's so bad about that?* He thought to himself. Plus, he also thought with the information he had, there could be many benefits he could reap if he took it to Jol. He had a lot to offer Jol. He knew the whole setup, inside out. He was the second in command in East Sockton, and there was hardly a secret he did know. *Jol would HAVE to accept me. I am valuable.* He thought. *But I will first have to weaken Koki's case. The socks are starting to like him around town.*

So Davet went on a mission to first sow seeds of distrust. He quietly kept spreading rumors about Koki. The town socks loved Davet. He was popular and very trustworthy. He organized the events and helped so many socks. The socks would turn to him whenever they were in trouble, and Davet would always come up with a solution and be there for them. For the socks of East Sockton, he was a friend they could always count on. That is what he used to spread all kinds of foul rumors about Koki, who had worked hard to gain a reputation and build trust.

Now that Davet had done a good job of spoiling Koki's name, his next step was to get a chance to talk to Jol and share his plan with him. He had tried many times but couldn't succeed. Since he was popular among the socks, whenever he tried to go out towards Warrenark, a sock would intervene, and he would have to return. But luck struck him one day when he was in Argylonia. He ran into a throwaway named Saon. Saon was a guard for Jol, and he wanted the same thing as Davet: a chance to prove himself to Jol. Saon and

Davet spent some days in Argylonia, coming up with various plans. Finally, they had one. The plan was that Saon would help Davet get a chance to talk to Jol, and when Jol would reward him for the information he shared and assign him a leadership role, he would appoint Saon as the leader of Jol's elite circle. It was Saon who worked to finally get a meeting with Jol.

Even though Jol had him detained when he arrived at Warrenark because of suspicions, he was still treated well enough when the guards of Warrenark realized that he was to betray the lost and switch sides. Finally, he now had a chance to prove himself once and for all.

Sal and Sol have been stationed at the mountain for a long while now. The surveillance was boring until one day, they saw something interesting. They saw a green sock in a cloak. It was a bit unusual from the others. None of the soldiers of Jol's elite circle looked like it. The cloaked green sock was giving orders at the throwaway camp, which made Sal and Sol realize that it was in command.

"That's unusual. A sock nothing like Jol's elite, giving commands!" Sal said, confused.

The cloaked green sock had a box with it, which it handed to another sock.

"Who do you think that is, Sol?" Garta asked.

Sol shook his head. "I'm not sure. But there seems to be a lot more activity down there. If it continues, we should report this to High Elder."

Garta agreed. Dart was working next to the mountain with Koki, setting up defenses. It was hot, and they were tired, yet Dart saw Koki smiling.

"What's that smile about?" he asked.

"Nothing. It is just you and me – teaming up again. I never thought I'd ever team up with someone. You are the only sock that teamed up with me ever. I guess I was wrong for always wanting to work alone. I just felt there would be issues with any sock if we worked together. But now that you are here, next to me, I'm glad that I have a teammate I can count on. At my side."

Dart just shook his head. "Listen, Koki, you have to stop thinking of yourself as a loner. You've accomplished so much. I have learned so much from you, and you are one of the best professionals I have seen. Your work speaks for itself, and everyone is glad to have you on the team. But you always let your past control your present and your future.

Tell me this. Do you like yourself, Koki? Have you made it so far by trusting yourself?"

Koki nodded.

"Then that's what matters. As long as you like yourself, the rest will follow. And I'll always have your back." Dart added.

"And I'll always have yours, Dart," replied Koki.

The two friends worked in silence after that, both reflecting on their lives.

Davet had reached the outskirts of town. He noticed there were more guards than usual. He approached two of them.

"Davet, welcome back!" said the one guard, enthusiastically wrapping Davet in a bear hug.

Davet smiled and then broke into laughter. "It was a much-needed vacation. But I'm back in time for the festival."

The guard smiled broadly. "You setting up a festival is exactly what the town needs right now. And now that you are here, I am sure we'll have a blast!"

Davet chuckled at that statement. *If they only knew*, he thought. "Well, anyway, I'll see you all later."

"Oh, Davet, just so you know, you do remember the two throwaways we caught?"

"Oh yes, I was about to ask about them. Where are they? We still have them, right?" Davet asked, alert.

"Yes, we have them alright. And we took them in for questioning," the guard replied.

Davet faked surprise. "Really? Why?"

"Crimes against East Sockton," the guard answered. "They are locked up."

Davet knew it had to be the safe house. "Well, thanks for letting me know that. Oh, don't tell anyone I'm back. I'd like to surprise them," he requested and winked at the guard.

The guards smiled. "Your secret is safe with us."

Davet walked away and made it toward the safe house. He looked up. It was getting dark. He knew he had to free the two throwaways as early as he could; he wouldn't get many chances. He reached the safe house quickly enough. He couldn't believe his luck. It was empty. *They are all probably at the festival*, he thought, *guess it's my lucky day*. Davet rushed to the holding room. Entering the room, he sees guards.

"Davet! Long time…When did you return?" the guards beamed. "Welcome back!"

Davet smiled. "It's good to be back. Who are these socks?" He pointed to the cell.

"Nage and Gamon!" The guard answered. "They are evil as they come."

"Really?" said Davet. "What did they do?"

"Yes, Crimes against East Sockton," the guard replied, "and they seem to think Koki is going to let them go."

Davet then had an idea. "Actually, good that you remind me of him. He wanted me to tell you two to go meet up with him on the other side of town. He's at his house. He needs to discuss some secret business. You might want to hurry; the festival won't be for long."

"But Koki said that we couldn't let them be unguarded," the guard responded, a little confused.

"Yes, he said you'd say that. He told me to tell you that something new has come up, and he needs to share some information with all the guards. I was the only one he shared this message with you know, since I still am the Vice Leader, and the place is on high alert. He told me to send all the guards as quickly as I could."

The guard looked down. "I'm sorry, sir, we shall leave right away. It's just that security is uptight!"

Davet nodded. "I understand, soldier. Don't worry. I am happy you are doing your best job. Now go, it is urgent. I'll stay with these two for a bit. Besides, Koki is sending more guards to new positions. Some kind of change of plan, I guess."

The two guards left. Once they were out of the safe house, Davet faced them. Reaching for the keys, he opened their door. Nage and Gamon looked at him, a little dubious.

"Come with me right now," Davet ordered looking over his shoulder to keep check. "Return to Warrenark. Jol is waiting for you two."

"And why should we believe you?" Gamon asked.

"Because I just opened up your cell door knowing there are two of you and just one of me, with no guards. And if you keep on asking questions, you can wave this chance goodbye and rot in this cell for the next hundred years. The guards will be back soon, just so you know."

Nage and Gamon didn't argue. They darted towards the back door, but Davet shouted and stopped them.

"Take the engineering exit. It will be easy to escape from there. Less guards and more grass around it to hide in. Plus, it is also the shortest route to the stables. You're not planning to RUN to Warrenark, are you?" Davet said sarcastically.

Nage ran back towards the engineering exit, patting Davet on the back while exiting. Everyone in and around the building was at the festival. They reached outside and ducked beside the building's fort wall.

Nage crept his head up, scanned the area, and then said, "Clear, let's go."

"Hurry up!" Davet whispered. "And don't forget to remind Jol, who helped you escape out of this place."

Gamon gave him a thumbs up, and they took off in the direction of the stables. Davet and the two escapees thought everyone was away. Davet thought he had done a great job of sending the guards away.

He was wrong.

One guard was never away as he was always working. Harf was famous for never leaving his post until the one who appointed him relieved him. Davet had completely forgotten about him. He noticed Davet was back and seemed in some rush. But he didn't know who the socks with him were. Harf had almost finished up for the day and was leaving when he saw Davet. He identified Davet instantly but couldn't make the other two out. Since it was Davet, he didn't inquire much.

He called it a day and decided to go to the festival. Leaving his office, he walked a few blocks to the festival. Harf wandered around for a bit, thinking what part of the festival to start with, and decided he was thirsty. He reached the stall and ordered a drink. While waiting for the drink, he noticed Koki.

"Koki," he called.

Koki turned and smiled. "Harf! You actually came outside," he laughed and remarked.

Harf smiled and replied. "Yeah, I heard there was some kind of celebration. I figured, why not show up? Anyway, I thought maybe I'd see Davet since he's back. I am sure he would have put together this festival. Have you met him yet?"

Koki looked at Harf quizzically and asked, putting his drink down, "What makes you think you'd see Davet? He's in Argylonia."

Harf shook his head. "No, I saw him about some hours ago with two other socks."

Koki was surprised. "Really? Two socks? Which means you cannot identify them? You know all of them there, don't you, Harf?"

"I do, but the two, I don't. I only know the socks in the building. I was about to question them, but they were with Davet, and one of them even gave a thumbs up to him, so I thought they were someone from the high office." Harf replied

"What did they look like, Harf?" Koki was now alert and had completely pushed his drink aside.

"One was green and yellow, and one was a gray and purple one. They were laughing," Harf replied.

Koki paled. "Davet was with Nage and Gamon!? Which way did they go, Harf?" he asked.

"Towards the stables, I believe. I am su…" Harf pointed outside the festival and was now very confused.

Before Harf could finish, Koki dashed out and scanned the area. He knew he had to find Davet. Something was wrong. Seeing Koki alarmed and tensed, Harf followed him out of the festival.

"Harf, can you please find Dart and tell him that I'm going to the stables? He should meet me there. And tell him to bring some soldiers. I am leaving right away." Koki requested Harf.

Harf, concerned, asked. "Is everything ok, Koki?"

"I'll explain later," Koki replied.

"Just find Dart." And with that, Koki ran off.

Harf started looking for Dart. Koki reached the stables shortly after. He saw Tella, a red sock, brushing the horses.

"Koki! Good to see …" Tella smiled.

"Tella, was Davet here recently?" Koki asked, interrupting Tella.

"Yes!" Tella replied. "About a few minutes ago. He was with two other socks. Never seen them two here before, but Davet sure did. He asked me to lend him two lint horses for them. I think they were his guests, if I remember correctly, from out of town. They went toward the outskirts that way," Tella informed, pointing west.

"Warrenark. That road leads directly to Warrenark!" Koki murmured to himself and then quickly turned to Tella. "Tella, give me your fastest lint horse."

"Sure, but… is everything okay, Koki?"

Koki had no time to explain, "No time to explain Tella. Fastest lint horse, now!"

Tella didn't make any further queries as the look on Koki told him there was some emergency. He quickly ran to the stables, pulled a lint horse out of the stable, and handed the reins to Koki. Koki ran, jumped, mounted that horse, and was gone in the wind.

CHAPTER 17
CONFRONTATION

Koki reached the outskirts of town, galloping the lint horse at lightning speed. He didn't understand yet what Davet was up to, but it smelled bad to him. *I really hope he didn't do what I think he did. Breaking those two out of jail is a recipe for trouble. Oh, Davet! What have you done,* he murmured to himself. He just knew, though, he had to stop him.

Meanwhile, High Elder was on the way to the safe house with her guard escorts. The festival had gone great, and for a long time in months, High Elder was in a jolly good mood. As she entered, she noticed that the place was eerily quiet. Even the guards were not there, despite all her new reinforcements. She knew that the guards would never leave their post, no matter the time or weather unless someone from the higher-up ordered them to. Instantly, she knew something was fishy. She darted to the holding area. With each step, her heart beat louder as she dreaded a jailbreak. She walked so quickly even the guard escort had to shift from walking behind her to jogging behind her. She pushed the holding area's door hard and stared directly at Nage and Gamon's jail cell. She stood there in disbelief! The room was empty! All the merriment of the festival washed away as she walked to the festival to double-check. The only thing she found in the cell was the nylon rope handcuffs that were used as shackles for Nage and Gamon.

She spun quickly to face her escorts, who were as surprised as her. They were also a little scared seeing High Elder so flustered.

"Does anyone know what happened? Where are the prisoners?"

Her roaring voice echoed through the large building.

"And where are all the guards!?" she shot another question at the escorting guards.

One of them was a high-ranking general. He was embarrassed as he had no answer to give.

"I don't… I believe they are at… the festi…"

"FESTIVAL? How can the entire fleet of guards be at the festival when two of the most dangerous socks were locked up in here!?" High Elder yelled, and the guard stooped his head.

"No, High Elder, we had our finest posted here to keep an eye on those two. I am sure there has to be someone on the inside who might have helped them. Someone from…" the other guard spoke.

"Someone from?" High Elder inquired, locking eyes on him.

"Someone from higher up the ranks. Someone trustworthy… We had given special instructions to all the guards posted here to take orders from no one other than someone superior to us. It doesn't seem like there has been an attack. Everything seems to be intact. Nothing is broken, which means someone the guards trusted might have come here."

The other guard, the high-ranking one, agreed and added, "That would be my conclusion too, High Elder. This doesn't seem like a break-in."

Instantly, a chilling thought zapped across High Elder's mind. *Did Koki let them out?* She questioned herself, *Could it be that he betrayed us all? Could it be that it was all part of his and Jol's plan? He is the only one who has gained our trust recently.* Horrifying thoughts came to her mind. It was the only thing that made sense to her at the moment. *Koki was a traitor, after all*, she thought. *Oh, what grave mistake have we made!*

Suddenly, she stopped, pondered, and realized there was another sock who had gained her trust lately. *Can it be*, she thought? *Can it be Dart?*

"Let's find out," she murmured to herself and turned towards the guards.

She pointed to two of them. "You both get some other guards, secure this place, and have this place searched and scanned. Check every nook and cranny. I want this whole place scanned in one hour."

The two guards nodded, saluted hard, and went running out of the holding area.

She then turned to the rest and, looking at the general, she ordered, "And please go find Dart immediately. Bring him here!"

Instantly, two guards ran out of the room to find Dart, leaving only two of the senior guards with High Elder.

"As for you two, continue to remain with me."

Both agreed and followed her as she darted out of the holding area to the tower.

The two guards who went to find Dart were racing towards the barracks when they came across a heavily built guard entering the barracks.

"Shoey! Wait up!" one of them shouted.

The heavily built guard stopped and waited for the two.

Panting and huffing, the two came to a screeching halt. In Koki and Garta's absence, Shoey was the acting leader of the guards.

"Shoey!" exclaimed the guards. "The High Elder needs us to find Dart immediately and bring him back to the safe house."

"Okay, okay, but what is the rush? You boys seemed to be scared witless. What is going on?" Shoey asked.

"The two throwaways … They are… They are gone!" One of the two guards said while catching his breath.

Shoey didn't waste time. He immediately ran into the barracks and dashed towards the common room. There, seated at a round table, were five guards discussing the games they played at the festival. Just as they saw Shoey running coming towards them, they stood up straight.

"I need you all to find Dart! Get him to the safe house immediately!"

"Yes, Sir!" they all said out loud in unison and dashed out of sight.

Dart was at a juice bar having a drink. The news of Nage and Gamon's jailbreak hadn't reached him. He had already been working with Koki to put up defenses around the city. The town looked happy and busy during the festival, but Dart and the rest of the team were working overtime to keep things in check and keep an eye out for Jol's miscreants. He was exhausted but was glad that he was able to play a role in the safety of the socks of East Sockton.

He was recalling the day's events and making plans in his mind for the next.

"After we are through for the day, I'd pay a visit to one of my associates' house. I have been keeping a network of socks, Dart, who help me from time to time. You need to learn to make one for you too. You need eyes and ears all over the place for the best security of the place, and you need to make friends with all kinds of socks for that," Dart was recalling Koki's words from a few hours ago when the two were out patrolling the town double checking the security measures.

"Noted," Dart had said.

Dart was impressed with Koki, as he had built a trust so strong no one ever questioned him. Even High Elder trusted him.

Dart was just about to order another when Bani, a guard, ran up to him.

With any his and hellos or salutes, he reported, "The High Elder needs to see you right away. Follow us."

Without hesitation, Dart followed Bani outside. There were some other guards there, all looking worried, which alerted Dart and told him something was up.

"What's going on?" he asked.

"The High Elder needs you back at the safe house right away. The throwaways, Nage and Gamon, the ones Koki caught, are gone."

Dart couldn't believe his ears.

"Where's Koki?" he asked, "has he been informed yet?"

Bani shook his head. "We don't know. We couldn't find him. High Elder sent us for you immediately!"

Dart hurriedly went to the safe house with Bani and the others. *This is dreadful! Nage and Gamon on the run! How could they possibly?* Thoughts ran through Dart's mind as he tried to figure out the next plan of action and plans of how to catch the two again.

They were at the tower. Usually, he would have to go to High Elder's room at the top, but this time, she was already waiting behind the door. As soon as the guards opened the door, he saw High Elder looking worried and angry.

"Dart! I need you to find Koki. I'm afraid he may have let the throwaways go."

Dart turned pale. "What?!" He exclaimed a little too loudly.

"Yes, difficult to believe, I know. But it all makes sense. Only a few of you are qualified to give orders to the guards, and there is no sign of damage, too, which means someone just walked in and let them out while sending the guards away. Davet's not here, and all of you were busy in one thing or the other. You were with him last time he was seen, right?"

"I was. We checked the security around the town. He posted me at the festival to keep an eye out, and then he left to meet some of his associates… and," Dart said, looking confused and surprised.

"And nothing. He was going to the holding area. No associates," High Elder interrupted.

"That would mean Koki turned on us," Dart said, still finding it difficult to believe what he was hearing.

The High Elder nodded. "I'm afraid that's the case. There's no other reason they could be gone. We have to act before they do some dama…"

Just then, Shoey arrived. He was out of breath. High Elder stopped.

"Shoey, what is it?" Dart asked. "What have you learned? Any news on Koki?"

"One of my guards just talked to Tella, the stable sock. She said Koki took off west toward Warrenark. He is after Davet."

"Davet? Did you just say 'Davet?' Davet's back?" The High Elder asked, astonished.

Dart shrugged. "I don't know. This is news to me."

"And you said Koki went after him. For what exactly? What did he do?" High Elder asked.

"I am afraid we don't have any news about that High Elder," Shoey responded.

"Then, let's find an answer to that before we start blaming Koki for a jailbreak of two prisoners he helped catch."

The High Elder thought for a minute. "Okay, fine, here is what you do," she said. "Dart, take Shoey and some guards and go after Koki. I still don't know what's going on, but we need him or Davet to clear things up. And we need to do this before news spreads across the town. We need to find answers and make reinforcements. Shoey, make sure we keep things quiet. Before you go, alert the guard stations that are set up to be on the lookout for anything suspicious. Anything that seems out of the ordinary, tell them to take action and investigate. If they catch someone or something, have them report it back to the tower immediately. And appoint someone competent to oversee them. I'll stay here. I don't want mistakes right now. Go."

She turned to Dart and said, "You need to solve this, Dart."

"I will, High Elder. I won't leave any stone unturned. I need to know, too, why Koki would betray us if he had. I also want to know why Davet didn't meet us when he came and left without telling. Something is definitely not right, High Elder."

"Yes, and we need to solve this quickly."

Dart nodded and left with the guards.

Suzy was heading back to East Sockton. When she reached Axall, she heard whispers of socks gossiping. It was something about a sock and a fight. She inquired to one group of old socks about what was all the gossip was about.

He said, "A terrific fighter is in town, kid. It wears a cloak, and no one can see its face. Best of the best. Nothing you would've ever seen. It took down the Elite Circle soldiers like they were toy soldiers. Alone. Can you believe it? And it was there for a box of some kind. Which I tell you, it took after it crashed all the soldiers. It was quick like lightning and strong. Something out of a legendary story, kid, you hear. Something is about to happen in the town for sure!"

Suzy didn't know what to make of the news about a scary cloaked figure. When she and the others reached East Sockton, they noticed the extra barricades and the increased guards.

"Something is about to happen in the town!" The old sock's words echoed in Suzy's mind after seeing all the reinforcements.

They quietly rode back to the safe house. Suzy, Arma, and Amawe dismounted their horses. She looked at the guards.

"You can go back to your barracks. Thank you for your help."

The guards waved and rode away. The three enter the safe house. They notice the High elder pacing around.

"What's wrong?" asked Suzy.

The High Elder looked at her. "Nage and Gamon. Gone. Koki may have let them out. Davet apparently is back, and Dart went with Shoey and some guards to find them."

"Woah! That is a lot of news. What happened? Koki, you said, he broke them out? Wasn't he the one who helped us catch… Wait, did you say Davet is back?"

"We are only assuming about Koki since he was the only one who could have made things happen given the circumstances. And yes, Davet is back. Koki is after him." High Elder said with a sigh.

"Okay, this is a lot to take. What do you need us to do?" asked Suzy.

The High Elder nods and orders her, "You go to Sal and Sol. Tell them what is happening. I'll be out that way shortly. What happened in Axall?"

Suzy shrugged. "Apparently, some cloaked sock beat up all of Jol's guards and took a box. That's all we were able to find."

The High Elder looked thoughtful. "Maybe a possible ally for us… But a cloak, you say, why a cloak."

"We have yet to find out. Guess we will know when we meet it."

"Yes. This is a riddle for later," High Elder agreed, "Thank you for going there. Now, get down to business." she added.

. Suzy left to meet Sal and Sol.

Koki figured that Davet must be going to Warrenark. He would have never believed that Davet was a traitor. But he just had to catch up to them. Determined, he rode on.

Davet reached Skipwell Pass. It was a shortcut that would cut a day off the trip to Warrenark. He remembered Sal and Sol showing him and Koki the layout. He remembered Sal almost tumbling to a great injury when they were mapping it. The whole area was covered by small pebbles and narrow paths. It was a dangerous trek, but Davet needed to save time and reach before he would get caught. He knew someone might have been following him for sure, as the news of jailbreak would surely have reached High Elder. Gamon and Nage looked at Davet.

"Why are we going this way?" Nage asked, a little scared.

"Because it'll get us there faster," Davet said. "Just keep going, trust me."

The three of them start making their way upward. Sometime after, Koki reached the crossroads. He could continue to Warrenark to the left or take Skipwell Pass.

"There is no way I am going back without catching that traitor and those two miscreants!" He said to himself.

He stopped and did some figuring out. He estimated that Skipwell Pass would be the shortest route to Warrenark and hoped he was right. Koki thundered down the road to the right.

When he reached Skipwell Pass, he scanned the surrounding area. Looking down, he saw something that resembled blown-away sets of hoofprints. He galloped his lint horse to them and started to see a whole track of hoofprints.

"Ah, yes! I am on track. You won't get too far, Davet. I am coming for you!" he smiled victoriously and steered the lint horse towards the track of hoofprints.

Meanwhile, Nage was getting tired of all the travelling. He was hungry and thirsty.

"Hey, Davet," he said weakly. "Let's stop to get a drink at least. I thought I saw a small stream," he said, pointing to the left.

Davet nodded. He, too, was thirsty and felt confident that no one would think of following them through the Skipwell Pass. "I think it's safe to stop for now. You two go get some water."

Nage and Gamon nodded. "We will bring you back some."

Davet looked around and found a tree for shade. He figured they were in the home stretch. He dismounted and decided to sit and rest for a moment.

"Finally, East Sockton will get what it deserves!" he muttered to himself as he sat under a tree, smiling mischievously.

He had barely rested when he heard someone shout his name. The voice sounded angry and was getting louder with each call.

He looked up and immediately paled as he saw Koki barging on his lint horse towards him. Jumping up, he starts to back away. Koki jumps off his horse in mid-gallop.

"What happened, Davet? Have you lost your mind? Why are you helping two known enemies of the lost?" He yelled as he came running towards Davet.

Davet turns and starts running. Koki dashed after him despite the rough terrain. Davet ran in circles, hoping the pebbles and the rocks would stop Koki, but he was wrong. He then ran in another direction towards the trees, but soon the path ended in a dead end. He turns and faces Koki, who was ready to take him down.

"You are a traitor, Davet," Koki said as he carefully stepped toward him, making sure to keep his hands up if Davet threw a punch or made a run for it.

Davet laughed. "Am I Koki? Look at you! You changed sides. What makes you so special, huh? Why can't I do the same."

Koki shook his head. "Because the side you are on is brimming with hate and anger. I chose a side that was peaceful, Davet. You are throwing your whole existence away if you join Jol. He will just use you."

Davet laughed. "You are a fool, Koki. Jol is going to take over, and I'm going to be on the winning side. I want more. I want to rule just like I deserve. The High Elder is content. I want to expand! Her way of life is in the past. I AM THE FUTURE," he yelled.

Koki pulled out some rope. "You have no idea how wrong you are. You don't know Jol like I do. But that is for later. Now, you are coming with me. Whatever you think doesn't matter. I'm taking you back with me to answer for your treachery. You can come in peace, or I can take you. Your call."

Davet just smirked. "You will not take me in. You can try, but you won't be able to."

Koki heard a noise behind him. He barely turned when he felt the hit of a club on his head. He instantly slumped to the ground. Gamon looked at the figure on the ground.

"That is for betraying us," Nage said as he hopped across Koki, who was down on the ground.

"What now, Davet?" Gamon asked, dropping the club.

"Throw him over the ledge. It's a huge drop to a pit. He will never get out. Right over there," Davet said.

Nage and Gamon picked Koki up by his arms and legs. Carrying him to the ledge, they toss him over the side. Davet looked and noticed large rocks under a huge pile of rock. He pried it hard, and after a few tugs, the rock moved. This created an avalanche of rocks, as all the socks came tumbling over the pit.

Laughing evilly, Davet walked off. *Take me for my treachery. Huh! Not happening.*

Nage and Gamon couldn't believe what Davet did as they stood stupefied. The three go back to their horses and ride off.

A few hours pass. The sun was setting, and only the whistling of the air could be heard. Suddenly, a few rocks scattered on the top of the pit shuffled. They stopped for a while and then shook again.

A hand finally punched one rock and emerged out from the rubble of rocks. It held the rope that was supposed to tie Davet. The hand threw the rope and pushed up, and out came Koki with bruises and dirt on his face. He gulped a gust of fresh air and pulled himself back over the ledge before crashing on the rocks again.

CHAPTER 18
JOL'S FIRST MOVE

Suzy and the others reached Sal, Sol, and Garta.

Sol raised his head from the maps he was reading to greet Suzy.

"Good to have you back, Suzy. So what happened at Axall? Any good news?" he asked with a smile which faded when he saw Suzy's worried expression. "What is it?"

Suzy shook her head. "I will brief you about that later, but first hear this. I have terrible news. Gamon and Nage escaped. And rumor has it that Koki may have something to do with it."

The other's jaws dropped. Sal, who was practicing with his staff, crashed on the floor when the staff hit his head. He stopped paying attention when Suzy said, "Gamon and Nage escaped."

"No, that cannot be," Garta tried to dismiss the idea as she found it unbelievable. "Koki would never turn back. He fought against them. He was the one who discovered about the machine they were building, remember?"

Sal shook his head. "But do you remember when Nage and the other one, what's his name? Gamon was caught? They said Koki would free them. Maybe they convinced him, or maybe they were not pranking, and actually, this was the part of the plan all along…" he said.

Sol was just standing there. "Well, I guess we have to possibly prepare to fight Koki," he said, picking himself up and his staff.

"And that is not all. We have someone new in the game. Someone deadly. Apparently, a cloaked figure. And IT is dangerous, enough to beat up a bunch of Jol's elite circle," replied Suzy.

"The Elite Circle, you say?" Sol confirmed.

"Yes, that too, a whole bunch, and we don't know anything about it."

Garta looked crestfallen. She sighed and said, making everyone curious, "I'm afraid we do know something. Follow me."

Suzy followed Garta to the observation point. Looking down, Suzy sees the cloaked figure in the distance moving slowly. She could see it was a tall, well-built figure.

"Oh no, we are up against a lot of odds! That seems to be it. The CLOAKED FIGURE!" she exclaimed.

Meanwhile, Dart, Shoey, and the other soldiers reached the crossroad that led to Warrenark. Dart stopped and thought for a minute.

"The pebbled route, Dart. It cuts the time to Warrenark. You can make it in almost half the time. But that is a secret route; not many know it, and it is difficult to go through it." Dart recalled Koki's words.

Would he go that way? Ah! He's Koki, of course, he would. He decided to take a chance. He turned around and addressed the others.

"This way will be dangerous. It's a slippery route. Also, we have to deal with the fact that we will possibly have to take Koki down. It sounds weird and dangerous since Koki is a trustworthy sock for many of us, but we have to be prepared for everything."

Shoey nodded. "If we must, we must."

Solemnly, they rode toward Skipwell Pass. Twenty minutes into their ride, they see a familiar sock limping slowly toward them. It was hurt badly. At first, everyone assumed a fighting stance, readying their staff. Dart went a little closer and, upon inspection, discovered it was Koki. He looked pretty beat up. Dart and the others dismount.

"Dart…Shoey," Koki smiled weakly and continued with his whisper-like voice, "I'm so glad to see you all. We don't have…"

Shoey cut him off and interrogated angrily, "Koki, why did you let Nage and Gamon go? We trusted you."

Koki shook his head. He moved towards them, stumbling, "I didn't. Shoey, you have it all wrong. It was Davet. I found out from Harf. Davet let them go. He's turned. Joined Jol's side. I chased after them and was hit from behind."

Shoey scoffed. "There is no way that is happening. Davet would never turn. After what he has done for East Sockton? He's a hero in our town. You traitor, how dare you accuse him. It's you who have been with Jol. We know this was your plan all along. We will take you in, and you will sit in the same cell you helped the two escape from!"

Koki dragged himself to Dart. "Dart, do you remember when we set up barricades? You don't believe them, do you? I need you to trust me. I need you all to trust me. Give me a chance, and I will prove it. Come on!"

Dart was conflicted. He was instructed to find Koki and/or Davet. Koki looked pretty beat up. *Why would he be on this road by himself? Why would anyone who he helped escape leave him thrashed and foiled like that?* He thought. He remembered telling Koki he would have his back, and Dart was a sock of his word. Also, he had worked with Koki closely and believed he deserved a chance. Taking a deep breath, he knew what he had to do.

Davet, Nage, and Gamon reached Warrenark. Jol and Chemi were there to meet them.

"Davet, you've done well," he said, patting Davet's back.

Chemi looked at Nage and Gamon and directed them, "You two don't look too beat up, which means you can still do the heavy work. Come with me. The weapon is all ready to use; it just needs a little cleaning up," she said. Nage and Gamon walked off with her after they were done with their reunion with Jol.

Jol looked at Davet. "We are preparing an attack on East Sockton in one week. This will be your final test. You WILL face your former friends, and YOU WILL fight. Am I understood?" Davet nodded.

"And one other thing."

"Yes, Jol?" Davet answered.

"You cannot afford to fail. You stay here until we ride." With that, Jol walked off, leaving Davet a little intimidated and nervous.

Unknown to Jol and the others, a quiet green sock was listening to everything from behind a bush. He blended so well with the plants that no one could see him. His name was Cam, and he was an old friend of High Elder. With everything going on, the one sock she knew she could trust was Cam. He was smart and a master of camouflage. He was one of the first socks she met when she appeared. She never mentioned him. He preferred it that way. High Elder had urged him, and now he was in Warrenark to listen and report. Without anyone noticing, he left to report to High Elder.

He arrived at East Sockton and delivered the grim news to High Elder without delay. The news shook her, and she immediately sent a guard to bring Garta back. Meanwhile, Sal and Sol were watching more socks going to the area down below. The cloaked figure couldn't be seen anywhere. Suzy, Arma, and Amawe started cleaning up weapons and getting them ready. The guard reached the lookout point and found Garta.

"What's going on?" She asked.

"Not good, Garta. Jol is preparing an attack."

"What! An attack? Do we know more? Do we know when?"

"In six days!" the guard replied frantically.

Garta immediately gathered the others, and she looked worried.

"Oh no, now what?" Sal shouted out.

"A possible attack is about to happen in six days in the town. We all leave for East Sockton immediately." Garta replied. "We regroup, and we take every soldier, and we fight. And we move today, now!"

Without much quibbling and questions, the group packed up camp and left.

Meanwhile, the cloaked figure was on the way to East Sockton. Twenty soldiers were escorting just to ensure it wasn't bothered. It wanted to see the town's outskirts. After all, Jol was paying. The cloaked figure had no allegiance. It didn't care about lost or throwaways. It just cared for itself.

It motioned for the guards to stop. "We will take a break for a few minutes," it said.

The guards didn't object.

Dart, Koki, and the others closed in on East Sockton. It took Dart vouching for Koki to prevent Shoey from taking him in. On the ride back, the others wondered if he was still truly on their side. They looked at Koki with suspicion. When they were about to enter the town, they were shocked to see the cloaked figure and the throwaway soldiers around the bend.

"Well, if it isn't Koki," said one of the soldiers. "I've been waiting to take you down for years. Your betrayal is not forgotten, traitor!"

The cloaked figure was intrigued. It was informed all about Koki from Jol. Koki, he was told, was perhaps its greatest match. Everyone got off their horses.

Shoey and the small group of soldiers were confused when they heard Koki being called a traitor. *Wasn't he on their side?* He thought.

He then looked at the cloaked figure, and when he recognized who it was, he remarked. "You were the one in Axall. We heard about you. Too bad you picked the wrong side."

The cloaked figure laughed. "I work for a price. I do not care about the lost or throwaways. Just me."

"You won't be laughing in just a while. We are not like the ones you thrashed back there!" Shoey replied scoffingly.

Just then, Dart walked up. "I know you have been told we are enemies. I can tell you one thing. That Jol wants to imprison all socks that aren't on his side," he said. "He doesn't want socks to be free."

"Listen to Dart!" shouted Koki, "I have worked with Jol; he won't spare any of you if you even think of being free!"

The cloaked figure blinked under its hood.

"Why did that word "free" make it flinch? And why did that sock seem familiar?"

"Well, Koki, you feel lucky? Are you now free, serving these town-folks who call you a traitor!" asked the one soldier.

Koki slowly limped up. "Even in the shape I'm in, I can handle you."

"Well, let's do this," the soldier yelled, rushing at Koki. Koki was injured and barely able to sidestep, but he was able to succeed and throw a spinning punch from behind that met squarely with the barging sock's face. The sock folded. Koki was about to fall but was saved by Dart, who helped him steady himself.

All the throwaway soldiers charged. Shoey and his guards met the charge. The sounds of staffs and shields echoed throughout the area. The fighting was intense. Staffs crashed into shields and with other staffs. It was a rumble. Two socks jumped on Shoey's back, grabbed him by the neck, and tried to bring him down. Shoey was almost down by the two throwaways when Koki came running and dived on one of the socks, prying him away from Shoey. Koki was bravely in any condition to battle, but he kept fighting on. He quickly got himself up and knocked down another three socks.

The cloaked figure thrashed three of the lost's soldiers, moving at a blitzing speed. It picked one and tossed him on two others who were barging towards it. Another soldier swung his staff at It, but he side-stepped, and before the soldier could raise the staff again, he hopped closer and punched him in the guts. The soldier crumbled and retreated.

The lost fought as best as they could, but the throwaways outnumbered them. Koki knew the cloaked figure was the one to take down. If he was completely healthy, he would have downed it already, but now that seemed a far-fetched idea. He felt no one with him could take the cloaked figure down, so he thought that he had to try.

Koki called it out. "Pick someone your own size, will you!"

The cloaked figure smiled and walked towards Koki. They met in the middle of the fighting. They slowly circled each other, eyes fixed on every move. Koki was watching the steps of the cloaked figure, which were cautious and stead. It suddenly jogged in one direction, stopped, and then threw a high kick, which Koki deflected with ease and flung it on the ground hard. It quickly recovered, spun around, and threw a low kick. Koki jumped and jabbed it on the way up. It was surprised, impressed at Koki's skill even in this condition. Koki immediately grabbed its arm and flipped the cloaked figure over his shoulder. With a kip-up, it quickly got its feet under itself. It replied Koki with a punch to his already sore side. Koki grunted in pain but wasn't ready to give up.

Meanwhile, Dart was fighting a throwaway when he noticed the soldier Koki downed earlier getting up. The soldier ran at Koki. Koki saw the soldier and deflected his attack, but It was running in his directly too. It took advantage of a distracted Koki, quickly ran, slid under him, and wrapped the hands around Koki's neck. Koki fought, trying to pry open its grip but he was weak. The cloaked figure tightened the chokehold. Koki's knees folded, and he went down, gasping and throwing his arms for air. Dart quickly dashed in their direction, jumped, and landed a knee on the cloaked figure's face. It didn't see Dart coming and was taken by surprise. It grunted in pain and let go of Koki, who dropped to the ground.

"Jol will imprison you too! All of you! No sock will be free," screamed Dart, "Don't you understand!"

He went for another punch, but the cloaked figure grabbed his hand, twisted it, pulled Dart toward itself, and hit him with a straight arm. Dart went heads down, legs up. The cloaked figure ran towards Dart and was about to kick him in the guts but suddenly hesitated.

Why was he so familiar? And why did that word free come up again? It thought.

It froze for a moment as it started having visions. He saw Dart in those visions but couldn't make anything of the place he saw or why it was envisioning things. Just then, the fighting soldiers heard galloping lint horses coming from a distance. It was Garta, Sal, Sol, Suzy, and a team of soldiers marching towards them. The throwaways saw the reinforcements, and the ones that were able to quickly mount lint horses took off. The cloaked figure was about to pounce on Dart, but one soldier intervened.

"Not now. We will take care of them later! We will have a chance soon!"

The cloaked figure grumbled, pushed the soldier, but knew he was correct. He mounted his lint horse, and before Garta and the rest of the soldiers could reach them, he rode off into the dust.

CHAPTER 19
THE LOST COUNTERS

Sal, Suzy, and the others didn't give chase. They were more concerned about Dart and the others. They all dismounted their horses.

Upon seeing Koki, Garta immediately acts. "Tie him up," she said, pointing to Koki. "He must answer for letting Nage and Gamon go."

Dart shook his head. "Garta, no. Koki had nothing to do with it. It was Davet!!"

Garta shook her head. "No way Davet would do that," she replied. "He LOVES East Sockton and never liked the throwaways. He didn't even like Koki because he is a throwaway." Garta was quick to make sure the others were reminded of what Koki was. "Plus, Jol is preparing an attack."

Koki and Dart stared in disbelief.

"At least we have Koki captured," Garta finished.

Shoey stepped forward. "Koki just battled the cloaked one and the others. He could have ridden off with them."

Koki then spoke. "I was at the fair when Harf, the engineer, told me he saw Davet with them. Also, Tella can back up my story. I was simply chasing them down when I was ambushed by Davet. You MUST believe me."

Garta paused. "Well, let's confirm that," she said. "We will take Koki to the outskirts of town." She looks at Shoey. "You will watch Koki while I, myself, verify this."

They reach the outskirts of town. Garta rides off. Sometime later, she comes back with Harf. Going up to Koki, she releases him. "I'm sorry Koki. But I couldn't take a chance. I already had High Elder alerted about our mistake."

Koki nodded. "You did fine," he said. "You and Shoey go back to the barracks. Start having everyone gather their weapons and stand by. We'll meet tomorrow at Palms Clearing."

Garta and Shoey nodded and rode off. Koki looked at everyone. "We should report to High Elder," he said.

The ride to High Elder was somber. Koki rode ahead of everyone else. Sal and the others felt bad. They were mad at themselves for even doubting Koki. No one said anything. They reached the safe house. Going in, they see High Elder. She smiled for the first time in days.

"Jol is preparing an attack, and we must be ready." Koki nodded. "I have Garta and the others rounding up soldiers."

The High elder nodded. "Also, the whole town knows what is going on. I already sent socks out with the message for everyone to be prepared," she said. "A lot of socks are scared."

Koki nodded. The High Elder dismissed all of the other soldiers out of the room, leaving only Dart, Suzy, Sal, Sol, and Koki. "You all are my most trusted socks," she said. "War is here, I'm afraid. We will take every soldier with us to the North Mountains to that encampment. Jol is gathering all of his soldiers, including his elite circle. We cannot afford to lose."

Everyone nodded grimly. She then looked at Koki. "I'm sorry for doubting you."

Sal, Sol, and Suzy echoed her words.

Koki nodded. "About that, I've given everything to our group that I could. I trained soldiers, followed EVERY order without question. And still, I wasn't trusted. I was tied up and escorted back to town. I was treated like garbage. It was as if anything I did to this point didn't matter. It's bad enough that socks in this town don't trust me, but when the socks I am closest to don't trust me either, that hurts! Except for Dart, I feel no one will ever fully trust me. After I take Jol down, I'm leaving."

"But Koki," High Elder began, but Koki held up his hand. "It is my decision." With that, he left the room.

Everyone just stood there, shocked.

Suzy slowly shook her head. "What have we done?" she mumbled.

Sal and Sol felt equally as bad.

The High Elder sighed heavily. "All this time, we thought Koki couldn't be trusted. And it turned out we betrayed the trust he had in us."

Dart was shocked. He knew he had to talk to Koki but now was not the time. Koki was in a different mood right now.

Sal spoke up. "Koki has the soldiers meeting up outside of town by Palms Clearing in the morning."

The High elder nodded. "We will all meet in the morning then. I suggest everyone get some sleep if you can."

They all then leave.

Koki was in the barracks. He spoke with Garta and Shoey. He opened up a map that Sal and Sol had made of Jol's encampment area. "You two are my most skilled socks he said. We will wait for Jol to show up. We will do a trident attack. Jol HAS to come through the side of Skipwell Pass. We will have three groups. Groups A, B, and C. Garta, you will command group A. You will go to the west of the pass and wait for a flag signal. Shoey, you will command group B. You will go to the right up the middle and make sure you are seen by Jol's soldiers. Draw them in. When they are near the bend, Garta will take group A and charge up the right. Then I follow with Group C. Am I understood?"

Garta and Shoey nodded.

Garta then spoke. "Koki, I'm sorry again for not trusting you. You taught me to never take a chance." Koki nodded. "That is why I'm not upset with you, Garta. Or you, Shoey. However, I feel other soldiers don't trust me. Therefore, when we win, I am leaving. You, Garta, will take over the soldiers with Shoey taking your position."

Shoey was shocked. "Koki, you can't leave," he said.

Koki just shook his head. "It's my final decision. You both are dismissed."

Garta and Shoey leave. Koki sat alone in his room. He sighed heavily. He really liked everyone, but he had too much pride. He then thought of Davet. Davet was largely responsible for this whole mess. All this time, he was the traitor. Not him.

The next morning, Dart and the others met up. They then rode to Palms Clearing. Koki was there with all the soldiers. Just then, there was a gasp from the crowd. Sitting atop a regal lint horse, High Elder rode up in battle gear.

Koki approached her and saluted. "What are you doing here?" he asked.

She smiled and dismounted. "My place is with my group and my other socks," she said. "What kind of leader would I be if I didn't show up? Besides," she chuckled. "I am no stranger to swinging a staff."

Koki nodded. "We are ready."

The High Elder nodded. "I will address them."

She climbed up a large rock. "Everyone, please stand next to me."

Dart and the others flanked the high elder on both sides. The soldiers went quiet.

She looked at the crowd. "Today is a grim day. We are facing the greatest threat to us. The throwaways are starting to gather for an attack on our town. You all trained for this day. Our very way of life is on the line. I hoped this day would never come. We CANNOT and WILL NOT let Jol win. He wants to rule us. We have every right to be free as throwaways. Today, we make a stand and defeat our greatest threat. WHO'S WITH ME??"

The soldiers all cheered. When the crowd quieted, High Elder spoke again. "Koki is my TRUSTED soldier. We follow his lead!!"

Dart and the others noticed she emphasized the word trusted. Koki just looked straight ahead. Dart wondered if High Elders' words had any effect on him. If they did, he didn't show it.

"Alright," Koki said. The crowd hushed. Koki stood for a moment, then spoke loudly. "WE WILL MARCH TO WITHIN 2 MILES OF THE ENCAMPMENT. THEN WE WAIT FOR JOL! GARTA AND SHOEY WILL LEAD 2 GROUPS." He then lowers his voice and looks at Garta and Shoey. "You two know what to do. Take your groups. You know the plan."

Nodding, Garta and Shoey start marching. They had two days at least to reach the encampment. Koki turned to the others. "Dart, Suzy, Sal, and Sol. You stay by High Elder. Keep Arma and Amawe with you." He looked at High Elder. "I respect you wanting to fight, but you are too valuable to get captured. The town needs a leader."

No one could argue with this logic. They all nodded and left for the encampment. The time seemed to fly by for Dart. He didn't know why he was so nervous. But he made sure not to show it. After all, Koki was in good (if not in full) health, his friends were nearby, and they had the advantage of a surprise.

By early morning of the second day, they came within two miles of the encampment. A scout rode up from Shoey's group to find out when he was to make a move. Koki set up seven socks between his and Shoey's group. When the time came, the signal would go down the line to advance. Koki and the others took a deep breath. The time to defend their way of life was coming.

CHAPTER 20
THE THROWAWAYS ADVANCE

That morning, Jol was in his chair staring out the window. The sky was cloudy, and an occasional thunder would strike, making the mood more menacing for the events to come. But the thunder didn't scare Jol; it only made him more eager and excited.

Chemi was gathering all the soldiers in formation. Murn and some other promising fighters were part of the group. And, of course, the cloaked one. It, however, didn't mingle with the group, so he waited in his own room, practicing with the staff. Just then, a guard came into the room. Jol looked up.

"What is it?" Jol asked. "You better not give me bad news!"

"Mafu is back," the guard said, trembling.

Jol gave a small smile. "Mafu? About time he came to his senses. Bring him in," Jol ordered.

Nodding, the guard left the room. Minutes later, he returned with three other guards who escorted Mafu, who looked beat up and tired.

Jol looked at Mafu and smirked, which made Mafu shiver. Mafu, after the time he had spent with Jol, had learned that whenever

Jol smirked, it meant he had something dangerous going on in his mind. He was scared of the punishment he might receive.

"Get Chemi here immediately," Jol instructed a guard while fixing his gaze on Mafu and then addressed him calmly. "Well, what are you doing here, Mafu? You certainly are courageous," his eyes narrowed, "or foolish. I will bet on the second one."

Mafu stood straight and, with a small and weak voice, tried to say something in defense, "Jol, I was loyal to you, and the only thing I ever wanted was to be your second. Your vice leader. But I think my methods were wrong, and I am here to correct them. I fully understand now that Chemi will always hold that position. Regardless, I still am loyal to our cause, and I know that you need help for your upcoming invasion. You didn't banish me officially. I hope you will accept my offer and take me back in. I will prove myself to you yet again. I promise you, Jol, I will fight for our cause till we win. I only ask you to forgive me and let me prove my loyalty again." He sounded desperate.

Jol thought for a minute. "Before I make my decision, let's see what Chemi thinks. If she agrees, consider yourself lucky."

Just then, Chemi walks in. She looked at Mafu and smiled. "Mafu... Mafu... Mafu. You aren't so mighty now! You wanted my position all along and even tried to blackmail Jol. What do you want now? And don't tell me you are here to MAKE THINGS RIGHT. You know what you did was foolish, don't you? And I think you know what we do with betraying foolish socks in our ranks."

"He wants to rejoin us," Jol answered. "The question here is whether he is useful to us or not. After all, we have all the muscle we need. The one sitting in the barracks alone,"

Chemi nodded. "Oh, so he now wants to fix things? Huh!" She thinks for a while. She didn't trust anyone easily, and Mafu had already broken the trust once, but she also knew they could use any help now as the army was about to walk into battle. She pauses and thinks for a while.

"Okay. You get another chance to prove your loyalty. But remember, you betray us again, and I will personally deal with you before Jol does." She growls and looks fiercely at Mafu, who looked relieved after hearing about another opportunity. "I will never trust you, so I warn you to just don't cross me again," she added.

Jol sat back down. "Well, you are in luck today. But don't think that you will be granted mercy again and again. You pull another stunt like you did and banishment will be the LEAST of your problems. I think you have worked with me long enough to know that I…"

"Don't forgive traitors and have the fiercest punishments for them, I know, Jol. Trust me, I won't disappoint you again!" Mafu said with a much louder voice than before.

"Very well, go to the barracks. You will report to Murn. He is now in charge of the Elite Circle."

Mafu nodded and left the room.

Later in the day, Jol went outside the gates of Warrenark. All the soldiers were in formation.

Chemi came up to him. "We have every able-bodied sock turned into a soldier here, Jol. We are ready for anything." She seemed proud and ready, but under her skin, she was anxious.

Jol nodded. "Much appreciated, Chemi. Never had a doubt! Stand next to me." Jol climbed up on a stone formation. The soldiers all quieted and waited for him to speak. "The time has come, my fellow Soldiers! Time to reclaim what has been rightfully ours!" Jol addressed the crowd. "We will show the Lost that their way of life is wrong. OUR WAY IS BETTER!"

"THE LOST HAVE LOST THEIR WAY! THE LOST HAVE LOST THEIR WAY! THE LOST HAVE LOST THEIR WAY!" The soldiers cheered.

Jol waited for them to quiet down. "We will NOT be denied our right! WE ARE THE THROWAWAYS!!"

"HAIL JOL! WHO SAVED US ALL! HAIL JOL, WHO SAVED US ALL!" the crowd starts chanting in Jol's praise.

He motioned for the crowd to quiet down again. "We will march to our encampment outside of town. But beyond that, we have to move carefully. We will surround East Sockton and slowly move in. WE WILL CRUSH ANY SOCK IN OUR WAY! We will break it into three sections. I will lead one. Murn will lead another. The last section will be led by Mafu."

The soldiers suddenly started booing. They couldn't understand how Mafu, the traitor, can be allowed to lead again. Jol quieted the crowd. "Don't you trust your leader? Have I ever betrayed you?"

"We do. No, you haven't!" the crowd responded.

"Mafu has mend his ways. He has pledged his loyalty again, even though he was foolish. You will follow his orders. TRUST YOUR LEADER!" Jol shouted, and everyone cheered his name again.

He walked to the front of the group to give the final order but stopped because he felt something wasn't right. *Maybe you shouldn't march at this time, Jol,* he thought but quickly dismissed the thought from his head.

"MARCH!!" He bellowed.

"ALL HAIL THE THROWAWAYS!" His army started marching, chanting all the way. Chemi walked next to Jol. She always knew this day would come. She saw it in Jol the first time she saw him wandering around. Chemi felt as if she nudged Jol in this direction. But she did not even know what to expect. She looked around and found Davet in the crowd.

"What do we do about him?" she asked, nodding in Davet's direction.

Davet was looking straight ahead, marching in unison. Jol started to think. Davet certainly wasn't loyal. He gave Chemi so much info about East Sockton. He looked over to the cloaked one. Just then, Jol had an idea. An idea that was sure to work.

Koki set up his sleeping bag, then sat down next to it with his head down. No one really said much to him. Even High Elder kept her distance. Dart walked up to him and put his sleeping bag next to Koki.

Dart sat down and shook his head.

"Why the headshake?" Koki asked.

"Because you are being stubborn, Koki," replied Dart. "These socks need you."

Koki snorted. "They need me, but they don't want me, Dart. There's a difference."

"And you will let them decide for you? You are a strong sock, Koki. Strongest I have seen and met. Look at what you have done so far. You have given East Sockton a fighting chance. You have trained them, made them strong through your training. And when it is time for you to be strong again, you are giving up on them? Or better yet, us. You are giving up on us. Some socks that know you and trust.

And maybe this might be the last time you have to be strong. Maybe after you defeat Jol, things will be different. They might see you for who you are. An honorable sock, a soldier, a leader, and most importantly, a friend we can always count on. Do you wish to give up on all of this? You never know, Koki. I know it is difficult to forgive when someone treats you like this. But only those with a strong mind and heart can bear it. And you are the strongest sock I know."

Koki put his head down but listened to every word of it. It might have influenced him but he didn't show. "Maybe, Dart. I need to think," he replied.

Dart understood. He patted Koki on the shoulder. "For what it's worth, I'll always have your side." Dart walked away.

He saw Sal and Sol. They were with Suzy. "Well, what did he say?" they asked in unison.

"Well, all I can say is that I tried. We have to give him time," Dart replied. "We will see." With that, they settled down for the night.

The next morning, Koki walked the ranks. The mood was somber. Every soldier was silent except for some murmuring. The High Elder motioned him over. Koki walked up and saluted.

"Yes, High Elder?"

"At ease, please. You don't have to be a soldier all the time. Walk with me, will you?" she replied. "I've been thinking a lot lately. And as you know, I feel as guilty as anyone for doubting you. You know that. But understand one thing, Koki. I never once doubted your heart and your intelligence. And that was what I feared. I know you are angry, and you have all the right to be, but I want you to understand my position. From where I sit, I have to calculate everything cautiously. Doubting becomes a part of you. And right now, you might be only paying attention to the idea that I doubted you. But I have simultaneously believed a lot of things good about you, too, which has made me question my own doubts at times."

Koki listened intently but didn't say anything.

High Elder continued, "A lot of what we have is because of you. We have an army because of you. Plus, we never knew that Davet was spreading lies and doubt. He has built a lot of trust and used that and your old reputation to defame you, making socks think he was one of us. That's what the majority think of you, Koki. But the truth is that with this whole upcoming battle, we need you. And this is also something that I have believed. This battle can make things right. This will define who you are once and for all. This day was bound to come sooner and later. Embrace all of this! And overcome. And you have my word; I will stand by you!"

Koki nodded and managed to say, "You are a wise sock."

The High Elder smiled, "It comes with age."

Just then, there was a shout down the ranks. Jol was close. This was it.

CHAPTER 21
A SURPRISE REVEALING

Shoey was visibly shaking, not out of fear but out of the anticipation of the fight ahead. He didn't want to fail because he knew a lot of his friends' and fellows' lives were at stake. He knew that the throwaways were fierce and better trained than his own army. Now that he had to lure them in, he had to make sure that he didn't make a mistake. His group remained hidden in the bushes and trees and waited for his signal before the bend.

They heard the throwaways get closer. Shoey held his hand up. The socks understood what Shoey was going to do. The plan was to distract them and take them by surprise. He moved away from his team and then came out from behind a bush and walked toward Jol and his army on the other side of the bend. Just as he was about to turn around the bend, he saw a sock dressed in battle gear marching his way.

"What trick is this?" Jol said to himself. "You don't scare me, you stupid LOST! Your tricks won't work," he smirked.

Shoey held up his staff and pointed at Jol. "You have no business here, Jol. If you are as smart as they say you are, you might want to turn back now! The Lost are way more prepared than you think they are. They are ready for whatever you have against them."

Jol smiled slowly. "Well, well, if it isn't Shoey, the staff slinger! Am I right? That's your name. I remember hearing about you. What do you think you can do?"

"Well, EVERYTHING. You have no idea!"

"You don't scare me, soldier! And if my plan is working, which I know it is, by now, Koki has captured your friends." He sounded proud and thought he would take Shoey by surprise.

But Shoey shook his head. "Koki is loyal to us, not you. Your lies won't work with me."

Hearing that, the smile on Jol's face wiped out. Suddenly he felt that his plan isnt that effective after all. He composed himself, looked back at his forces, and then back at Shoey, "Well then, Shoey, be prepared to face pain."

He started advancing toward Shoey. Shoey waited till half of the forces was behind the bend and half of it was across. This created a big gap, and Shoey saw it as a chance to take action.

"NOW!" Shoey yelled. "ATTACK!"

A whole shadow of rocks and staff covered the sky and momentarily darkened the sky. The hum of rocks filled the air. All the rocks and staffs rained down on Jol's forces, taking them by surprise.

CRACK!!! THUD!!! THWACK!!!

Jol's forces were confused and chaotic. They quickly raised their shields as rocks kept showering on them from behind the bushes.

"GET THEM!!" Jol bellowed.

His forces ran toward Shoey's group. Shoey quickly retreated and ran where his forces had sheltered behind the bushes and dived. Jol thought he was running away and scared, so he decided to go after them. He plunged ahead. Just then, Garta jumped from the side bushes, leading the forces, and charged right into Jol's group.

She swung her staff and swept three socks along with it, sending them flying and crashing and knocking another group of socks that were marching toward them.

"This was easy," she giggled. But as she turned around, she saw Mafu coming her way. He had his eyes locked on her, and he started running in her direction, knocking every sock in the way. Garta didn't wait and started to run towards Mafu. They met in the middle and she swung down her staff. Mafu crisscrossed his hands in front of him, and when Garta's staff landed on his arm, it cracked. Mafu smirked, and without a second's delay, she lifted her up and was about to toss her into the crowd of fighting socks when Garta jerked and knocked a knee in his face.

"Ow!" Mafu growled. He threw her down.

Garta landed, balanced, and, with a hard leg sweep, knocked Mafu down. Just like that, the fighting became more intense. Shoey, on the other hand, was grappling and fighting three throwaways at once. He tossed one, grabbing him from the shoulder and swinging him into the crowd. Another sock threw his staff at him, which he quickly caught mid-air and threw it back. The staff went struck straight into the stomach, sending the sock flying and knocking three more of his comrades fighting behind him. Then Shoey slammed the other on the ground. They weren't the best Jol had to offer, but fighting three socks was still too much. Shoey was panting heavily but was alert and ready. He dashed towards Murn, who was marching in Garta's direction. Behind Murn, Jol was fighting with a heavy-set sock. The heavy-set sock was tall and well-built, and his actions were quick. But Jol was quicker. He ducked when the heavy-set sock threw a kick and quickly recovered. He already had his hands up to block the punch the heavy set rock threw at him. Then the heavy-set sock threw another punch, which Jol first dodged, and before the sock could throw another punch, Jol's arm dragged him and thrashed him on the ground. Mafu saw all that, but since he was marching towards Murn, he could react quickly. But then he saw Jol readying himself with his staff, which had a sharp end, to finish off the sock. Shoey steered in his direction, and Murn followed him. Before Jol could bring down the staff, Shoey leaped and lunged and dived in Jol's direction. Murn tried to intervene in his leap, but Shoey was too strong. He slammed into Murn, throwing him off the feet, but it only slowed the dive a little bit. He grabbed Murn mid-air and then shoved him in Jol's direction. Shoey and Murn together crashed into Jol, sending him rolling on the ground and saving the heavy-set sock's life.

Shoey immediately recovered and jumped on Jol's back. Jol was a much bigger sock, though, and barely moved. He crashed his back into a rock wall. Shoey groaned in pain and fell to the ground. Jol turned and kicked him in the head, almost knocking him unconscious and groggy.

"So much for your preparation, Lost!" he chuckled.

Grinning, he plowed forward toward the town, tossing, throwing, and punching any sock that would get in his way.

"Going somewhere?" a voice called him out.

Jol stopped as he recognized the voice too well. "Ahh, finally! The traitor's back! I am gonna enjoy this!" he called and turned around with a mean smirk on his face.

Koki stood with his forces, eyes fixed on Jol. He had waited long for this. Without further ado, he leaped into action with staff raised over his head and dashed toward Jol.

Garta was still fighting with her forces on the other end. She took down two throwaways. One of them landed right next to Shoey, kicking off dust into the air. A few rocks and pebbles bumped on Shoey's head, waking him up. He opened his eyes and couldn't see clearly at first. He could only hear a THWACK here and CRASH there. Groaning, he slowly stood up, tried to focus hard but couldn't, and thus, fell back against the wall. Suddenly, among all the loud yelling and fighting, he heard a voice he instantly recognized.

"You are a mad sock, Jol! You don't want to free these socks. You intend to keep them as slaves!" Koki yelled and swung his staff down.

Jol stretched his staff under Koki's and swiveled it hard, sending Koki down spinning. Koki quickly kipped up and was ready again.

"You don't know anything traitor. These socks don't know any better. I know they cannot be trusted with freedom. There is no freedom out there."

"Just because you didn't have a good life doesn't mean others have to go through the same, you tyrant. I used to believe in you, but when I saw darkness in you and called you out, you banished me. But I won't let you do the same with the others. You tyranny end today, now!" Koki yelled. Anger could be heard in his voice.

"You fight for those who don't even trust you! You are more stupid than I thought!" Jol giggled.

"You might spread all the rumors about me, Jol. And these innocent socks might even believe you and think of me a traitor. But you have not and will not succeed. I have a few friends who believe in me. A few friends are good enough for me against a tyrant like you!"

Shoey rubbed his eyes hard to help him focus. He saw Koki swinging in every direction. Some blows landed on Jol's staff; others missed him by small distances. Shaking his head to clear the cobwebs, he finally could see clearly. He decided to get up and lend

Koki a hand but saw Mafu making his way towards Koki, planning to take him down from the back. Without a second's thought, he charged toward him. Mafu saw him coming and turned just in time to deflect Shoey's attack. He jabbed his staff forward twice, then up. It was a classic move that might have worked on a lesser sock, but Shoey wasn't one. He easily deflected it easily and even turned it around. With a quick helicopter spin of his staff, he knocked Mafu on the head, sending him sliding into the dirt and gravel, leaving him unconscious.

Dart and the others could hear the fighting in the near distance, but they thought it was more important to stay close to High Elder. The High Elder was visibly shaken and worried. She wanted to be out there on the battlefield, but Dart and others suggested that they couldn't afford to lose her and needed her leadership. Just then, they heard a sound. A loud bang. They ran toward the front. There was a big cloud of dust, and at first, they couldn't see anything. Even the clacking of the staff and shield couldn't be heard, as if the fight had settled. But when the dust cloud settled, they saw a lot of socks down on the ground. Many were in pain, coughing, and crouching.

Then, about a hundred yards away, the cloaked one came out of the bushes.

"Well, if it isn't the leader of the Lost and her…. friends!" it exclaimed, facing Dart.

Dart and the others raised their weapons.

"You don't know what you are doing," yelled Sal. "This is not your fight."

The cloaked one smiled. "Oh! But it is. It is my fight more than you think it is, soldier. I'd give you this opportunity to save yourself and run. All of you."

"Well, that is a bit of a problem. We don't know how to give up!" Sal replied.

With that, the cloaked figure charged, staff in hand. It quickly hit Sal in the legs, knocking him down. Sol had charged the same time and swung his staff, but the cloaked sock had anticipated that and ducked in time. Without even getting up, It swept the staff and pulled Sol's feet, which brought him smacking down on the floor. Next, it struck Suzy's arm with the staff and quickly attacked Arma and Amawe. It moved the staff like a paddle, left and right, knocking each of them with each swing, sending both Arma and Amawe rolling on the ground.

"It is quick!" Amawe whispered to Arma.

"We have to attack it together!" Arma replied.

These socks were special in their skill but weren't seasoned fighters, and the cloaked one was. Within no time, with a series of kicks and a few swings of its staff, it knocked the entire team down. Then, it advanced to Dart.

Dart stared at it. He was alert and ready, but he noticed that It wasn't much scared or nervous. As if, it was a day's job for it.

"I'm telling you to stand down!" Dart tried to warn it. "A lot of socks will suffer if you keep this fight on! You don't have to. You don't know Jol. He isn't what he says he is. He is not a leader."

"You think I care? Care about that lunatic? He is of no use to me. I just wanted to get to you, and he was good help. That's all." It replied and charged. It ran forward at blazing speed, with an upward swing, and was standing right in front of Dart before its sentence was complete. Dart was barely able to get his staff up in time. After one strike, the cloaked one somersaulted back to dodge each swing of Dart's staff. When It was at a sufficient distance, and Dart had stopped swinging his staff, the It one charged again. It moved right, then left, and spun in the air for a strike. Dart couldn't quite track its movements. It jumped high into the air, shadowing Dart with the big cloak, staff raised over its head, and as It landed, It brought down the staff hard on Dart. Dart was taken aback by its sheer skill and wasn't able to react. Its staff struck Dart on the shoulder hard, which sent him rolling down on the ground. Before Dart could recover, It raised the staff again for a second blow, but by this time, Sol was able to deflect its staff by darting his own in its direction. It fell, recovered itself, and immediately somersaulted back.

It stared at Dart, planning and plotting another attack, when something suddenly flashed into its head. It completely confused it, as if it was seeing a whole different world in front of Itself. It saw a room, just like other visions. Seizing the opportunity, Suzy attacked, kicking It in the back, interrupting its train of thought. The visions disappeared. Dart, too, saw an opening and quickly swung his staff, striking its legs and tossing It off the ground. While in air, Dart kicked it hard in the stomach, which sent her flying and rolling on the ground for quite a distance.

"Stand down, and you won't be hurt. You don't have to fight for someone else!" Dart called.

The cloaked figure was hurt bad. Still, it got up, but the hood had flown off. Dart's jaw dropped at what he saw. He didn't expect what he was seeing. As more dust settled, it heightened Dart's amazement as the cloaked figure's features became more and more visible.

"It can't be what I think it is," Dart whispered to himself, still finding it difficult to process what he was seeing. He focuses and takes a closer look – His eyes widen. "Oh, Dear! That cannot be true! Is it her? It's the same… Same color… Green Color, the same she had… and those diamonds, the three red diamonds on the top! IT IS HER. IT'S DA…" Dart was talking to himself, and with every little thing he noticed, his amazement and surprise made his heart pound faster. The staff from his hand dropped and rolled, but he was frozen where he stood.

The dust had now settled, and It and Dart could see each other clearly. She suddenly grabbed her head as, when he clearly saw Dart, memories came rushing to her mind. She could hear Dart playing and singing. Soon, other voices could be heard.

"Whee!! Whee!! Here I come. Watch your back! Jet's is on the way…" One speeding sock said.

Then she heard and saw Dart and herself looking at the stars in the night sky, and they both were saying, "Free!". Then, a strong throb of pain passed like a wave in her head as she saw one final memory where she was on her knees crying. Then it hit her.

"DART!! You... you are Dart! Aren't you?"

Upon hearing her say his name, Dart experienced a pain in his head too. He also started seeing so many flashbacks. They wouldn't stop. He screamed in pain, sinking to his knees.

"Darla…" he muttered before passing out. The High Elder and the others just stared in confusion.

Meanwhile, Koki was getting tired as he was already injured and yet was fighting Jol, who was a tough warrior to fight with. He looked around and saw that his forces had downed and tied Murn as four tall, well-built socks in armor were towering over him. He saw Mafu throwing a jab at Garta, who dodged it with ease. She didn't look much tired, which surprised Koki, but he knew that Garta was a warrior unlike any. Garta ducked and, quickly recovering, punched Mafu in the stomach, then an upper hand, then with her staff, flung Mafu across the field, sending him flying into a small unit of Mafu's forces, which crashed. Mafu tried getting up but couldn't. Garta helped her own soldiers up and quickly separated her flank and Koki's.

Jol was seeing all this dismayed. He couldn't believe that he was losing despite having an army so huge. "How can this be?" he muttered, sounding helpless.

He then looked at Koki, who had his hands up and was smiling. "You are losing, Jol. It will be wise to give up and surrender now!" he shouted.

Jol knew he was right about losing, but he was in no way going to surrender. He pondered for a moment and then decided to do what he never thought he would do. He shrieked a loud call, and his soldiers started retreating. He signaled Murn and Mafu, who came and joined him. The three looked at Koki, who was now joined by Garta and a whole unit of soldiers with staffs at the ready behind them.

"We'll come some other day, boss," Mafu said.

"Yes. We. Will. Mafu. Yes, we will," Jol repeated.

With that, he gestured to his forces, who started retreating. Murn stopped for a bit.

"But the cloaked one, boss, what about it? The Lost have captured it," he asked.

"I don't think it is of any use to us anymore," Jol replied without much worry.

All three started their way back to Warrenark.

When the forces were at a safe distance, and Koki was sure that Jol would not launch a surprise attack, Koki congratulated everyone, thanked and praised Garta, and said, "I must get back to High Elder."

Without waiting for a reply, he ran back to High Elder but was immediately confused at the scene in front of him! Sal and Suzy were holding a sock bound in chain, on her knees. Dart was in a sitting position and seemed groggy, surrounded by High Elder and Sol, Arma, and Amawe, who were talking quietly.

"What did I miss?" Koki asked.

The High Elder looked up. "Apparently, these two, Dart and the cloaked one, seem to know each other. He called her Darla!! Has he even mentioned anyone to you by the name Koki? He fainted after calling her name – must be some long-lost memories!"

Koki looked clueless. He first took a step towards Dart, thought for a moment, and then went to Darla. "How do you know him?" he interrogated.

Darla looked up. "He's my… He's... my… mate." Her voice trailed off, and she slumped forward again.

"Mate?" Koki echoed. "But how?" He waited for the reply, but Darla seemed too lost, sad, and angry to reply. He walked over to Dart. "Dart? Can you hear me?" He asked, speaking as loudly as he could.

"Yeah, yeah. I can hear you just fine. I am right here, not in Warrenark!" Dart replied, smiling.

"You know that sock?" Koki asked, smiling, relieved that his friend was fine.

"She is my mate," he replied.

"But how can this be?" Koki asked.

The High Elder sighed. "I've never heard of this before! I've never heard of a sock finding their mate. I don't even remember mine."

"Me neither." Sal and the others echoed her statement.

Koki was still in shock, but he shook it off. "High Elder, Jol is retreating; we have to end this. We can solve my riddle later."

The High Elder nodded her agreement. "You should go now. Are you up to it?"

Just then, Garta came back and informed, "Jol's forces are scattering. But not even in the direction of Warrenark!! We have won!!"

Koki shook his head. "Not while Jol is loose. If he is retreating, he might have some other dangerous plans. We HAVE to go to Warrenark and end this once and for all. Go find Shoey," he said to Garta.

"We have to go right away." Garta nodded and ran off.

Koki looked at Dart. "Dart, are you up for it?"

Dart slowly got to his feet. "Yes. Yes, I can Koki."

Koki looked at Darla, who was unconscious. He nodded. "Very well." He looked at the sky and estimated the time. "We leave in a few hours."

The High Elder motioned for Sal and Sol to carry Darla. Koki went off to find horses. Arma and Amawe followed, leaving Dart and Suzy behind.

Suzy looked uncomfortable. "Dart," she began, "You know what you mean to me. We had so many happy times." Tears formed in her eyes. "And… and…I don't want to lose you…but she's your mate, and I will respect that and respect you if you wish to…"

Dart's eyes moistened. "Suzy, I don't know what to say. I don't know what to do!" He replied, sounding helpless and confused.

Suzy wiped her tears, looked up, and smiled. "I know what you should do. Be with her, Dart. This never happened before. Not to any sock. It's like a miracle as if it's meant to be. We can still be friends."

Dart nodded. He walked closer. They held each other. "Just one last thing, Suzy, we will always be good friends. You can always count on me to have your back, you know that, right?" he said. Suzy nodded. Together, they turned towards the forces to prepare for action one last time.

CHAPTER 22
THE FINAL CONFRONTATION

A few hours later, High Elder and the others regrouped. "This is it, everyone. I am sorry I won't be following you guys as he, the cloaked one, Darla, is confined as a precaution."

Dart nodded. He wanted to stay behind and talk to Darla. He had so much to ask and so much to share, but that had to wait.

Koki looked at everyone. "It looks like it'll be me, Dart, Sal and Sol, Suzy, Garta and Shoey. That's is it, right? Did I miss someone?"

The High Elder nodded. "I sent Arma and Amawe to find their contacts to get any info about Jol. I want all remaining guards to stay in East Sockton. It's confirmed that Jol and his assistant Chemi are on their way to Warrenark with a few others. It seems everyone else scattered to the hills."

Koki looked at everyone. "Mount up! We leave in 15 minutes."

Just then, he slumped to one knee again. The others rushed forward.

"Are you okay?" asked Sol.

Koki nodded. "I got hit with a rock. It'll pass." He got back up.

Everyone mounted their lint horses and rode off. Early next morning, Jol was in the courtyard pacing.

"How can this happen?" he bellowed.

Murn and Mafu stood speechless.

"Surely they will come here," said Chemi. "We should retreat and regroup."

"No!" he yelled. "I will NOT leave Warrenark!"

"THAT IS THE ONLY THING YOU SAID RIGHT EVER, JOL!!!" a voice yelled, which was followed by a mean chuckle.

Jol looked up, surprised at the confidence in the voice. He saw Dart entering the courtyard, followed by Koki and the others.

"Koki, you traitorous lint dog," Jol growled. "So, this was your goal? To take me down?"

"Well, yes. Actually, part of my goal. I also wish to show these innocent socks that you rule, that you are nothing but a tyrant, and that you will never let them have a free life where they can live the way they want," Koki replied angrily.

"You will fail, traitor. But let's go for it. Let's do it, Koki. You and me. No one else!!" Jol yelled, rage audible in each word he said.

Dart looked at Koki. "You don't have to do this alone. This is suicide. You are hurt; you are tired. We are here to help you. We stay together, fight together, and win together."

Koki shook his head. "I have to, Dart."

Mafu, looking to further redeem himself, then spoke up. "Let me take him down, Jol."

Jol nodded. "What are you waiting for then, Mafu? You can…CHARGE THEM!!" He yelled, running forward.

Koki and the rest charged too. Murn dived and tackled Suzy, and both of them went rolling on the ground. Shoey quickly ran and grabbed Murn from behind, lifted him up over his head, and tossed him away.

Garta and Mafu squared off.

"You are nothing, Garta!" Mafu hissed.

"We'll see about that. Let's not waste time talking – unless you want to ask me to go easy on you," she replied, swinging her staff. Mafu met the swing with his own staff.

Koki and Jol slowly circled each other. "Let's see if you still remember everything I taught you. Hope you still got it, Koki, because I am all out of mercy now."

They locked up with each other. Meanwhile, Dart was analyzing the situation and the place. He figured if he could take Chemi down, Jol might back down. He darted in her direction, but Chemi saw her coming, and she was quick to back away, holding her staff in front of her.

"Leave me alone," she screamed!

"I don't mean to hurt you if you will just listen. He is lying to all of you..." Dart tried explaining.

"And you are telling the truth? You expect me to believe you."

"Just give me a…" Dart was trying to say something, but Chemi charged with her staff and him. He saw her coming as she wasn't much of a fighter and easily dodged her. He snatched her staff from her and slowly tapped her behind her knees, making them buckle under her. She tried resisting but Dart quickly took a rope and tied her. He motioned Garta to look after her and then ran off to fight alongside Koki.

Jol and Koki grappled with each other. Even though Koki was hurt, he found new strength to fight Jol because of his anger. In no time, he had the upper hand, slowly bending Jol backwards. Then he spun around behind him and wrapped his arm around Jol's neck. But before he could choke him, Jol elbowed Koki in the ribs, flipped him over his shoulder, and slammed him on the ground. He raised his leg to stomp on Koki, but Koki sprung to his feet. But all the flipping, slamming, and spinning took its toll, and suddenly everything became a blur. Koki staggered and found it difficult to keep his feet under himself. Jol saw the opening and quickly landed a punch on Koki's jaw. Koki crashed to the ground.

Sal and Sol ran to help Garta. Mafu didn't notice Sol crouching behind him, but Garta did. She advanced with her staff, dashing as fast as she could to force Mafu to walk back instead of running aside. He tripped over Sol and fell to the ground. Sal wasted no time, leaped forward, and punched him in the head with everything he had. Mafu collapsed like a sack of potatoes.

"Ow!! My hand," Sal yelled. "I think I'll never be able to write again."

"You are a righty anyway," said Sol.

"Well, yeah, but maybe I was going to learn to use my left hand! You never know…" Sal replied.

Sol just chuckled. "Quit kidding around. The team still needs our help. Let's go"

Jol saw Shoey take Murn down. Mafu was tied up and struggling. Garta, too, had Murn face down in the dirt and was tying him up as he tried to break free. Koki, by now, had landed quite a few punches on him. Two in the stomach, three on the face. He was tossed and thrown two times and nearly missed being choked. He knew he didn't have a chance against Koki, and if someone else joined him too, he would surely be overpowered. He quickly ran from the courtyard and ran into a tower and started lowering the gate. Dart was quick to follow but was a good distance away. He ran as fast as he could, but the door was already halfway down and closing fast. He knew he wouldn't be able to make it if he kept running, so he heaved himself and slid. He slipped with closed eyes, and when he stopped, he heard a loud thud and chain ringing. He peeked with one eye and saw that the spike of the gate had jabbed into the floor and missed the thread on his head by a mere centimeter.

"Don't get killed today, Dart! Please!" he whispered to himself.

He sighed in relief but then suddenly heard yelling as if someone was giving orders. Getting up to his feet, he heard Jol shouting orders to someone. The tower had doors and stairs going in different directions. He looked around frantically.

He saw Jol on top of a wall in between towers. Looking down, he saw Koki and the others. They had Murn, Mafu, and Chemi tied up. Jol called out to Koki.

Koki looked up. "Jol, you coward. Come back and finish this."

Jol cackled. "Oh! I will finish. But in a different way." He motioned.

Just then, Nage and Gamon appeared pushing a large wooden thingamajig. Koki and the others paled. It was the MACIIINE. Jol had finally put together the SOCK-KILLING MONSTER!

Together, the two turned a hand crank. Slowly, a table started rising. Koki gasped. A sock was tied on the table, and his arms and legs stretched, making him look like a giant X.

"That's Davet!" Garta gasped.

His mouth was bound. Jol motioned for the gag to be removed.

Davet immediately began yelling. "Koki!! I'm sorry for betraying you. PLEASE SAVE MEEEE!!"

Jol cackled and yelled back, "And you thought I was going to let you go. Ha! It should be Koki on that table, but I'm not that lucky." Looking back at the others, Jol continued, "This is what I do to traitors. Look and learn Koki. As soon as I eliminate Davet, I'm leaving. But just temporarily. I'll be back, and then it will be you on this table!"

"Ummm, I don't think so, Jol," said a familiar voice.

Jol turned around. It was Dart. Everyone in the courtyard looked up in disbelief.

"Dart! What are you doing?" Suzy screamed.

"Oh no, no, no! He thinks he can take Jol head-on alone? He is out of his mind!" Koki remarked, visibly scared for him.

The whole team wanted to jump into action but knew that if they played smart, Jol would immediately use the machine on Dart. They had to be careful.

Dart gulped. He was able to fight, but Jol was a warrior, among the best of the best – and he was much bigger. He wasn't Koki or Garta or Shoey, for that matter.

Garta shook her head. "It should be one of us up there, Koki. Jol won't show mercy. You know that."

Koki was shaken. "All we can do is hope Dart has what it takes," He replied hopelessly.

"Well, Dart, Aren't you a little too brave? I underestimated you. I will give you that. Didn't count you in my plan." said Jol. "But I guess eliminating you will be the added bonus, and I will be able to execute my plan again."

Dart balled up his fists and put his arms up. "You talk too much, and you sound awful! How about we end this already?"

Jol motioned to Nage and Gamon.

"Start it up." Nage pulled a lever. Gamon smiled at Davet. The timer began.

Jol started explaining to Davet, who was scared out of his wits. "Every 5 minutes, a pebble drops. In 30 minutes, you will feel a tug. And then you go bye-bye! So, you have six pebbles to watch. If you try to untie yourself, it bypasses the pebbles. Bye, bye, traitor!"

Just then, Gamon fell to the ground, and Nage, who was on the edge, fell all the way down from the tower to the ground below. Jol turned around to see what had just happened. Arma and Amawe were there.

"But how do they always appear," Dart muttered with an ear-to-ear smile. Amawe, without wasting any time, looked at the machine and said. "We have to figure it out. Harf showed me how to shut it down."

Jol charged at Dart. Dart tried to dodge, but he was too slow for Jol. He barely moved out of the way. Jol pivoted and whipped his foot out, catching Dart in the leg. Dart went down. Jol quickly leapt on Dart and sat on his chest, pinning his arms down. He punched Dart in the face. "How does it feel losing, Dart?" He punches Dart again.

Dart groaned in pain. The others down below could only stare in horror. Meanwhile, Arma and Amawe were still trying to stop the machine. Dart wasn't fighting back, nor was he trying to get away from Jol.

"You are dumber than I thought you were, Jol. I cannot believe how you even became a leader. You are the dumbest sock I have met in my life!" Dart laughed despite the pain. He wanted to keep Jol engaged, to keep him distracted, buying time for Amawe and Arma.

"A pebble fell. HURRY!" yelled Davet.

The words infuriated Jol, and he started punching harder. "How am I dumb when it is *You* that have lost, Dart?" said Jol, punching Dart again. Dart laid still.

Arma looked over. "I have to help him. He won't last long!"

Amawe understood and said, "I'll keep going; you go save him."

Arma ran and jumped on Jol and kneed him in his back. She knew she had no chance, but she had to try. Jol grunted in pain and surprise but quickly got up and elbowed Arma in the ribs. He quickly grabbed her by the throat and lifted her up, holding her with one arm. Arma clutched at Jol's fingers, but his grip was too strong. Chuckling evilly, he walks to the ledge. "Say goodbye to her. Here comes one of your PALS, Koki!" Jol shouted down below.

Koki and the others gasped. Meanwhile, Amawe kept working. Another pebble dropped. Davet shook his head, tears forming in his eyes. "Forget about me, Amawe. Go help Arma. Tell everyone I'm sorry for everything I've done."

Dart opened his eyes and heard Arma struggling and grunting. Slowly getting up, he saw Jol holding Arma over the ledge. Shaking the rest of the cobwebs from his brain, he ran and grabbed Jol from behind, squeezing him as hard as he could, causing him to drop Arma on the edge.

Jol looks at Dart. "This time, you won't get up," he hissed. He elbowed him on his face, which loosened Dart's grip and sent him staggering back. He quickly turned, yelled out, and charged at Dart again. But this time, Dart was ready. He crouched down, causing Jol to fall over him and Dart to slip from his hand.

Everyone down below cheered. "Come on, Dart, you have this," Koki whispered to himself.

Dart ran, jumped, and landed both knees into Jol's back. Jol fell to the ground face-first. Before he could get up, Dart jumped on him and punched him several times in his ribs and back. Jol smacked his fat hand on Dart's face and knocked him away. Wheezing heavily, he staggers to his feet. He swung again at Dart, but Dart ducked and then followed with an uppercut, catching Jol flush in the jaw. Jol stood there wobbling. Dart backs up a few feet.

"This is where your story ends, Jol." Before Jol could understand what was going on, Dart ran at him, jumped in the air, and punched Jol with all his remaining strength in the eye. Jol wiggled, tried staying on his foot but failed. Everything in front of him became a blur, and even the words and cheers from down below sounded like slurs as he crashed to the ground. More cheers broke out from below. Dart ran over to Arma and Amawe. There was one pebble left. Davet was crying and mumbling.

"I think I got it," yelled Amawe triumphantly.

"Let's cut him loose," said Dart. "But you do have to answer for your crimes. Deal? Or I can leave you with this machine."

Davet frantically bobbled his head agreeing. He was brought down from the table, and Arma quickly tied his hands behind his back. Then they tied up Nage and Gamon.

"Let's tie up Jol too. We don't want him getting on his feet again," said Dart. They turned, but Jol wasn't there. They looked around and, when they didn't find him anywhere, walked down the tower stairs. Dart found the lever, and the gate rose. They walked out. The others were waiting. Everyone hugged Dart.

"You did it, man. That uppercut was the finest I have seen in a long time! I guess I am a good teacher," said Koki and chuckled.

"Congrats," Sal and Sol echoed.

"Jol disappeared," said Dart. "Did you see him run down here somewhere?"

"Nope. But that's fine. We'll get him later," said Koki, patting Dart in the back. "We have the others, and the throwaways have retreated. Let's just go home with the captives."

With that, they slowly walk out of Warrenark with Nage, Gamon, Mafu, Chemi, Murn, and Davet all tied together.

CHAPTER 23
THE AFTERMATH

They eventually reached East Sockton. It was sunny out. The town socks who were already awaiting them rejoiced and started merry-making and singing when they saw coming with almost all the captives. Dart and the others had done it for the town, and the town sock were happy. They defeated Jol and the throwaways. Things were looking bright. The threat was over. They handed over the prisoners to Garta, Shoey, and some other guards. They then went to the safe house. Inside, High Elder was waiting for them. She smiled, and they all hugged. They all immediately felt as if a great weight was taken from their shoulders. Koki was especially proud of Dart. Dart was the hero. He defeated Jol, after all, which was not a small task, given that he was almost twice his size and a more practiced fighter. They would figure out what to do with the others.

Then, High Elder addressed the obvious. "What about Dart's mate? This never happened before. What does it mean? How did you remember?"

"I don't know," said Dart. "I guess it was when I looked at her directly. Others out there might have their mates in our world. Again, I don't know. And I know she is a prisoner, but I will request you, High Elder, that I at least am allowed a word with her."

Sal nodded. "Well, if I never find mine, I'm happy being with Sol and the rest of you." Sol high-fived him. "Me too. Except your snoring. Don't do that, please," he replied.

Suzy smiled. She was happy with where she was with Dart. She was just glad they talked. Arma and Amawe just then showed up.

"How did you get up there with me? You guys have to tell me your secret!" Dart remarked.

Arma just smiled. "We have our ways."

Koki stood up. "Dart really did a great job, and I did say that after Jol was defeated, I would leave."

The smiles from everyone's face faded. All looked embarrassed and sad, and their heads dropped.

But Koki had something else in his mind. He smiled a mischievous smile. "What's with the sad faces, friends? I said after 'I' defeated him. And I didn't; it was Dart all the way, and plus, Jol is still out there."

Everyone looked up with smiles cracked at each face. Koki winked. "So, I guess I will stay until the job is finished."

Everyone cheered and hugged him.

"Ok, Ok, enough," he chuckled. "We certainly need to question the prisoners, and Dart may want to talk with his mate."

They all nodded.

"She is in the barracks holding room," High Elder said, "not a cell. She did commit some crimes, so until then, we have to figure out a punishment."

Dart got up to leave. "Very well. I will see you all later." He left the room.

Dart practically ran to the barracks. He saw Garta. She went with him and opened the holding room door. Standing there was Darla. He walked up to her. She sobbed, and they tightly hugged.

"Oh! Dart, when I was told you were gone, I cried and cried. Jet and the others tried to comfort me, but it was no use. But when I came here, I had no memory, so I had to figure out how to survive."

"I remember Jet! He was the fastest one, right?" Dart exclaimed.

Darla nodded. "After I saw your face, it all came back to me. I guess I passed out and when I came to, I was here."

"It doesn't matter," said Dart. "I don't know where to even begin, Darla. We won't lose each other again. That much, I know. But how did you become such a great fighter?"

Darla smiled. "I went looking for you but got sleepy. When I woke up, I was in this world. I wandered around and ran into an old sock who taught me about this world and how to fight. I remembered you for a long time and made it a mission to find you. But over time, my memory faded, and I stayed in Socktopolis, making a living hunting down socks that owed debt. I heard about throwaways but never held an allegiance with anyone. I came out this way with some others and came across Jol, who hired me. And the rest you already know.”

Dart smiled. “I did say one day we would be free.” With that, they held each other in a hug and fell silent.

While the town was busy preparing for a festival for their victory against Jol, a boat slowly left Axall, in the dark part of the night, across the Parsal Sea headed to Lamillee, which was three weeks away. A sock rowed a paddle in the both with an injured eye and one hand. The other hand rested tightly on a box. The sock sat with its head down cloaked. He grunted which was a signal for others to paddle faster. They seemed scared. In the dark night, the gray color of the sock seemed dark black.

“Enjoy all you can, Sockton! This won’t last. I will be back, and this time, nothing will stop me!” The gray sock croaked and whispered. The gush of air pushed his hood, showing a blackened eye. “I am coming for you, Koki! I am coming,” Jol whispered in the night, getting his hood back on as he slowly smiled.

The End